"A man just doesn't work for a woman, Emily," he said without looking away from his task. "I have my pride."

"Oh, honestly." Emily gave a careless wave. "That's the silliest thing I've ever heard. You must be joking."

"No. I'm not." Jeremiah darted her a glance, then refocused on the task at hand. "I'll stay until the end of the month to teach you as much as I can about running the store, but then I'm moving on."

The thunderous drum of panic beat wildly within Emily's chest as she realized she might be fighting a losing battle. "But, Jeremiah, what difference does it make if you work for me or Tuck? It's the same job."

"It just matters, that's all."

TRACEY VICTORIA BATEMAN lives in Missouri with her family, which includes a husband who is a prison guard, one daughter, three sons, a Husky dog who would like to believe he is human, and a guinea pig who seems to think he is a dog. When not focusing on the enjoyable role of wife and mother, Tracey loves to read, cook, and play piano. She is also very involved in the music department at her church.

Books by Tracey Victoria Bateman

HEARTSONG PRESENTS
HP424—Darling Cassidy
HP468—Tarah's Lessons
HP524—Laney's Kiss

Emily's Place

Tracey Victoria Bateman

Heartsong Presents

Dedicated to:
My husband, Rusty Bateman.
You're my kind of hero, Honey,
And now you have it in writing.
Special thanks to my crit partners:
Nancy T., Chris L., Pamela G., and Tamela H. M.

A note from the Author:
I love to hear from my readers! You may correspond
with me by writing:

Tracey Victoria Bateman
Author Relations
PO Box 719
Uhrichsville, OH 44683

ISBN 1-58660-690-5

EMILY'S PLACE

All Scripture quotations are taken from the King James Version of
the Bible.

All of the characters and events in this book are fictitious. Any
resemblance to actual persons, living or dead, or to actual events is
purely coincidental.

PRINTED IN THE U.S.A.

one

1885 Harper, Kansas

Emily St. John pulled on the schoolhouse door with a firmness that wasn't quite necessary to close it. The finality of the action brought a smile to her lips. She fastened the lock and slipped the key into her beaded purse.

Turning away, she took a large gulp of fresh, late spring air. She couldn't help but be amazed at how much better the simple act of shutting out the responsibility and drudgery of teaching made her feel. Lord willing, that door wouldn't be opened again until the beginning of next term—not by her hands, anyway.

Her steps remained light and quick as she began the short walk to the mercantile. The grass looked greener, the prairie flowers more lovely; and it seemed as though the birds serenaded her, no doubt sensing her relief.

No more schoolchildren for months, she thought gleefully. Then a sudden touch of guilt wiggled inside of her. The problem wasn't the children at all, she had to admit, but their teacher. The last five years had proven the worst of her life.

The town nearly burst with pride when she'd returned from a year of training at Emporia Normal School with a teaching certificate to her credit—the only schoolmarm in Harper ever to attend school specifically for the position. It proved Harper, Kansas, was becoming a real town.

Emily figured it was just one more instance of life taking her where she didn't necessarily want to go. She'd gone because it was expected of her. An orphan, she was grateful that Aunt Cassidy brought her from Missouri to Kansas when Aunt Cass married Dell. The two had raised her as one of their own. She'd had a secure childhood filled with love and laughter, so who was she to throw that back in their faces by refusing to go?

Her maudlin thoughts invited the all-too-familiar heaviness to return, and she released a frustrated breath at her brief reprieve.

This summer she had another plan. She had every intention of joining Mrs. Thomas and her little band of suffragists. Though Emily had attended her first and only meeting out of mere curiosity, she had to admit, she'd been impressed and agreed with Mrs. Thomas—it was high time women were given the right to vote.

Emily glanced up, surprised that her thoughts had carried her so quickly to the mercantile steps. She opened the door and stepped inside while the bell dinged her entrance. "Good afternoon, Mr. Tucker."

"Afternoon, Granddaughter." Mr. Tucker's grizzled face brightened. After being a confirmed bachelor for most of his life, the poor man hadn't stood a chance when Emily's granny had taken a fancy to him. With the approval and well wishes of the entire town, they'd married a couple of years ago.

Their happiness was a bittersweet thing for Emily. Some folks thought reminding her of her new grandfather's age was a comfort—as though her Prince Charming might come along when she was seventy, just like Tucker.

Emily snorted at their ignorance. If Prince Charming wanted to wait until he was seventy, he could find himself a different princess.

"What was that, Missy?" Tucker asked.

Emily rose on her toes and pecked a kiss on his cheek. "Sorry, Tuck. Just woolgathering."

"Must not have been a very pleasant thought," he grouched. "I tell a girl hello, and she grunts at me."

"You're right. My thoughts weren't very pleasant, and I'm sorry." All she needed was for Tuck to run home and tell

Granny on her for being rude.

"Here," he said, pushing a jar of candy across the counter. "Have a licorice stick, and we'll forget about it."

Emily eyed the sweet temptation, thought to decline, then gave in and grabbed one. Why was everyone always trying to feed her, anyway? Disgusted, but knowing she'd better not make any noises for fear of offending her stepgrandfather, she attempted a smile at the old man. "Got any mail for us? I told Ma I'd pick it up after school."

"As a matter of fact, I do." He shuffled to the postal slots behind the counter and returned with a handful of mail.

"Thanks, Tuck. And thanks for the licorice." Emily turned to go, but stopped at the sound of Jeremiah Daniels's deep, familiar voice as he walked out of the storeroom.

"Hi there, Emily. Last day of school, huh?"

Her stomach flip-flopped as he sent an easy wink in her direction.

Wishing she could dry her suddenly damp palms, she found the presence of mind to give him a nod and respond. "Did you hear all the shouting when I dismissed?"

"Sure did. I imagine everyone else in town heard them too." He grinned broadly, flashing even, white teeth. "You leaving now?"

"I was just getting ready to, yes."

"Me too. I'll walk you out." He removed his apron and hung it on a nail next to the storeroom entrance. "I'm headed home now, Tuck. See you in the morning."

"Hold on a minute," Tucker said.

Jeremiah hesitated. "Yeah?"

The storekeeper cleared his throat. "I–uh. . . The thing is, I thought I'd take my wife on a picnic tomorrow." He pulled at his starched collar and averted his gaze to an imaginary speck of dust on the counter. "Think you can run the store by yourself?"

A grin played at the corners of Jeremiah's lips. "I think I can do that." He winked at Emily again, and her knees felt wobbly. "I didn't know you were such a romantic fella, Tuck."

The older man's face darkened to deep red. "Now, who said anything about bein' romantic? Ellen has a notion to eat outside on the ground. That don't make no one romantic." He shifted his outraged gaze from Jeremiah to Emily. "And don't think I didn't see him wink at you like you two was cookin' somethin' up. You best not go spreadin' tales about me, else I'll have somethin' to say about it. And that's the truth."

"I wouldn't dream of saying a word, Tuck," Emily said. "Besides, everyone already knows you're an old softy where Granny's concerned."

He released a loud breath. "Now, see? That's exactly how rumors get started. Don't you go repeatin' none of that gossip, Missy. You hear me?"

"You have my word." Emily grinned and opened the door. "Good day. And tell Granny I said hello."

Jeremiah followed her outside. He paused on the step and leaned close as though they were conspirators. "I guess we shouldn't tease ol' Tuck, should we?"

Emily's heart picked up at his nearness. "I suppose not," she murmured. "It upsets him for anyone to think he has a soft side."

"Can't really blame him, though. After all those years of evading capture, the man surrendered like he wanted to get caught. He never even saw it coming, and now he melts like ice in July any time your granny is within a hundred feet of him."

"Poor Mr. Tucker," Emily said, laughter bubbling to her lips. "Not only does he suddenly become a husband, but a grandfather to seven children and even a great grandfather, as well."

"Well, there's not much a man can do about it. When a woman sets her cap for him, he's bound to end up smitten. He might as well put on his Sunday best and head for the altar."

Emily gave a snort, then immediately regretted it as Jeremiah lifted his brow in a challenge.

"You disagree?"

What could she say now without giving away the fact that she'd had her cap set for him since they were ten and he hadn't "ended up smitten" yet?

"Yes, but let's not talk about it." She quickly descended the steps.

Jeremiah's boots thudded on the wooden planks as he followed her. "All right. Have it your way. How about walking with me to the livery, and I'll help you hitch your team?"

"There's no need. I'm walking home today. Ma needed the team to go see Laney. The new baby was born last week, and Ma can't seem to stay away."

"Girl or boy?"

"Another girl." Emily grinned. Her brother Luke—Laney's husband—earnestly prayed for a boy during each pregnancy, but so far, God had blessed them with three girls.

Jeremiah chuckled. "Maybe next time. Anyway, it just so happens that I had to bring the plow in to get it sharpened, so I have the team. Gives me an excuse to drive you home."

"Oh, really?" Emily tossed back her hair and sent him a saucy grin. "I don't recall you asking if I'd like a ride home."

He removed his bowler and pressed it gallantly to his chest. "May I have the honor of escorting you, Miss St. John? It would be a great pleasure, to be sure."

A giggle escaped her lips. "I would be pleased to accept your kind invitation, Mr. Daniels."

He grinned. "Shall we, then?"

The feel of his hand guiding her across the street sent an ache of loneliness and longing through Emily. Why couldn't he see her as more than the girl he grew up with? She'd loved him for so long, it had become a delicious habit—a dream she couldn't live without. If he could only see her the way she saw him, maybe the dream would become reality.

He squeezed her elbow and then let go as they entered the livery stable where he left his team that morning. "Afternoon,

Mr. Collins." He smiled at Emily. "I'll hitch up the team and be right back."

Emily nodded, wishing her heart didn't go into a tizzy at the smallest of smiles from Jeremiah.

Emily kept quiet and stayed out of the way while Mr. Collins finished grooming a gray mare. He finally straightened up with a grunt. Fishing a handkerchief from his shirt pocket, he swiped at his forehead and the back of his neck.

"You didn't bring the team today," he said, inclining his head toward Emily.

"I know. Jeremiah was kind enough to offer me a ride home."

His eyes shone in amusement. "Oh? You two finally courtin'?"

"No, Sir!" Emily's cheeks burned as she heard the forceful words leave her lips. "He only offered me a ride home, and I accepted out of politeness."

"And no one can argue with Emily's manners, can they, Mr. Collins?"

Emily turned at the sound of Jeremiah's voice. She couldn't determine whether it was wounded pride, hurt, or merely embarrassment that hardened his tone; but she inwardly cringed, knowing that whichever had prompted the steely glint in his eyes, she was to blame.

"Ready to go?" She tried to keep her voice cheerful. Relief coursed through her as his expression softened.

"I'm ready. I brought the team around front."

They bid Mr. Collins good day and walked out to the hay-scented yard. Once there, Emily accepted Jeremiah's proffered hand and allowed him to help her onto the seat. She stepped up, so conscious of Jeremiah that she was unconscious of anything else and failed to establish a firm step. The mail she'd collected from Tucker's flew from her hand and scattered to the floorboard and ground.

"Easy does it," Jeremiah said, placing his hands on either side of her waist to steady her.

Her cheeks burned mercilessly, and she settled onto the wagon seat, unable to utter a word. But that didn't stop her vicious, self-deprecating thoughts. *Stupid woman, stupid woman, stupid woman.*

Tears choked her.

Jeremiah gathered up the letters and dropped them in her lap. "Here you go." His chipper voice did nothing to improve her mood.

She looked up.

"What's wrong?" His eyes clouded in concern. "Did you hurt yourself?"

"No," she muttered, taking the pile of mail he extended toward her. She looked it over, pretending great interest.

He moved to the other side of the wagon and climbed onto the seat. After waving good-bye to Mr. Collins, he flapped the reins and the wagon lurched forward.

"Emily, about what Mr. Collins said."

"Yes?" she asked, still rifling through the mail, most of which seemed to be business relating to the ranch.

"The thing is. . ." Jeremiah cleared his throat. "You know Tuck is planning to sell the mercantile, right?"

Emily glanced up in surprise. "He is?" What had that to do with Mr. Collins's teasing?

"You didn't know?"

The wagon rolled out of town and onto the rough road.

"I had no idea. Granny never mentioned it." Her heart suddenly softened in concern. Was Jeremiah worried that he would lose his position should Mr. Tucker sell out? Surely, he should know by now that Tuck wouldn't just leave him in a lurch.

"The fact is. . ."

Emily was just about to abandon the rest of the mail so she could give Jeremiah her full attention, when the inscription on the next envelope captured her interest.

Miss Emily Sinclair.

Emily scrunched her brow. She hadn't been called "Sinclair" in many years, and the name looked unfamiliar and quite unsettling.

"Something wrong?"

She showed the envelope to Jeremiah.

He frowned. "Tuck gave you the wrong mail? That's not like him."

"No. This is me."

"I don't understand."

"Emily Sinclair. That's my name. At least it was my name a long time ago."

"I remember. You look so much like Luke I forget you're adopted." He grinned. "The same red hair and freckles."

Emily sniffed. "At least his hair turned dark."

"Your hair is cute," Jeremiah said.

Emily glanced back over the envelope and gave him a dismissive wave. "If you're partial to orange."

"Maybe I am. And green eyes. And freckles."

If only he were serious! She scowled. "Stop teasing."

Turning the letter over again, she started to tear into it, but hesitated. She supposed she should wait and let Ma open it. As if reading her thoughts, Jeremiah quirked his brow.

"Aren't you going to open it?"

"Shouldn't I wait until I get home?"

"Why? It's your name on the envelope. Sorta."

"I know, but. . .well, I suppose you're right." She grinned. "Besides I can't wait to see who would be writing to me."

She tore open the envelope and took out the letter, carefully unfolded it, and read aloud:

Dear Miss Sinclair,

My name is Andrew Cambridge, and I am the attorney for the Harrison estate. I trust this letter finds you well.

I must first bring you the sad news that your Grandmother Harrison has passed away. She died quite suddenly in her

*sleep several years ago, and her husband, your grandfather,
two years earlier.*

*We have been attempting to discover your whereabouts for
quite some time in order to inform you of the provision your
grandmother made for you in her will. As it has taken this
many years, the money was invested for you and has grown to
quite a handsome sum.*

*Please respond as soon as possible so that we may settle this
long overdue matter.*

> *Sincerely,*
> *Andrew Cambridge*
> *on behalf of the Harrison Estate*

Jeremiah released a low whistle.

Emily turned to him. "I didn't even know I had a Grandmother Harrison," she said, still trying to absorb the information that she had just inherited what appeared to be a tidy
sum from a source she hadn't known existed.

"You had a grandmother you didn't know about?"

"It seems so. I feel odd—like I should be sad or something,
and guilty because I'm not."

"You can't mourn someone you didn't even know."

"Why didn't they tell me I had a grandmother on my ma's
side? I always thought since Ma was dead, any family she had
must be too. Why do you think Aunt Cassidy didn't tell me?"

Jeremiah shrugged and shook his head. "I don't know, but
sitting here isn't going to answer any of your questions. I'll
drive you on home, and you can straighten all of this out."

"Thank you, Jeremiah. I'd appreciate it."

Emily read the letter over several times during the drive.
With each reading, her spirits rose. She wasn't sure what con-
stituted a "handsome sum," but perhaps this inheritance was
God's answer for getting her out of the schoolroom. Why, she
could travel or enter the university, only. . .or. . . What had
Jeremiah said? Mr. Tucker was selling his store? She vaguely

remembered a conversation with Granny about Tuck selling out and resettling in Central Kansas to be near Aunt Olive and her family. The question was. . .would Tucker sell to her?

She sat up a little straighter on the wagon seat. With Jeremiah to run the mercantile, she would see him every day and he would never, ever have to worry about losing his job. And maybe all that togetherness would grow on him until he came to see her as more than the girl he grew up with.

She closed her eyes as if to will it to happen as she'd just imagined. This was her one chance. . .her one chance. It just had to work out!

two

Emily handed Mrs. Marshall two bits change and smiled as the older woman gathered her purchases and bid a cheery good day. Emily forced herself to remain where she stood until the bell above the door dinged the matron's departure, then she fairly flew around the counter and took up her entreaty once more.

"But why won't you stay on and work for me, Jeremiah?"

He shrugged, scowled, and resumed his duties without a word.

Emily followed him around the display of Healey's magic elixir. She stopped short of slamming into his broad back as he halted and began to fill in the gaps in the display.

"A man just doesn't work for a woman, Emily," he said without looking away from his task. "I have my pride."

"Oh, honestly." Emily gave a careless wave. "That's the silliest thing I've ever heard. You must be joking."

"No. I'm not." Jeremiah darted her a glance, then refocused on the task at hand. "I'll stay until the end of the month to teach you as much as I can about running the store, but then I'm moving on."

The thunderous drum of panic beat wildly within Emily's chest as she realized she might be fighting a losing battle. "But, Jeremiah, what difference does it make if you work for me or Tuck? It's the same job."

"It just matters, that's all."

Emily detested her whiny, pleading tone. And she shuddered to think what Mrs. Thomas would say should she hear the newest member of Harper's chapter of the Kansas Equal Suffrage Association begging a man to stay and work for her.

But the fact was—votes for women notwithstanding—if Jeremiah didn't agree to manage the mercantile, Emily might as well ask Mr. Tucker to return her money. Then she would have no choice but to hightail it back to the schoolhouse and resign herself to teaching forever.

She gathered a deep breath to steady herself for the next phase of the battle. "Be reasonable, Jeremiah," she said, trying without success to keep her voice even. "I need a good man to run this place. I counted on you to stay on as manager like you have for Tucker all these years."

He quirked a brow and flashed her a wry grin. "You shouldn't count on a fella without checking with him first." He pushed the last bottle into place and walked back toward the counter, stopping midway to straighten a display of dime books. "I'm happy that your real ma's family left you all that money, Emily. But just because you can buy Tucker's doesn't mean I have to stay and work for you."

Emily trailed after him. "Think of your poor mother, Jeremiah. What will she do if you don't have a job to support her?"

His lips twitched. "It's mighty thoughtful of you to be concerned about my ma, but rest assured I can still provide for her without your generous salary."

Heat suffused Emily's cheeks. "It's not very gentlemanly to make a lady beg and then laugh at her efforts." With a huff, she flounced around the counter and reached for the bolt of dress goods she had carelessly left out in her haste to resume her discussion with Jeremiah.

She spun around and lifted her gaze to the empty spot on the top shelf. A tremor slid down her spine, sending a shudder through her body. She hated climbing of any kind. Even short steps up. Emily preferred to keep her feet firmly planted on the ground where God intended for them to stay.

Warmth encompassed her elbow just before she heard Jeremiah's soft voice behind her. "Here, let me put that away for you."

Straightening her shoulders, Emily jerked her chin and climbed the small ladder, willing her hands to stop trembling. "I am perfectly capable of doing it myself." She swallowed hard, her head spinning from the lofty position three steps above the ground. With a firm grasp on the shelf in front of her, she drew a shaky breath and slid the bolt into place.

"Be careful stepping down from there," Jeremiah cautioned, grasping her elbow once more.

Emily jumped at the unexpected contact. A scream tore at her throat, and she tumbled from the step and into Jeremiah's strong arms. She glanced up into his startled gaze.

"Easy does it." He set her on her feet, keeping a steadying hand upon her back, the other around her wrist for support.

"Th—thank you, Jeremy." Emily stepped back quickly, smoothing her palms over her skirt. "I'm fine now."

"Jeremy? You haven't called me that since that time I stole a kiss at the harvest dance when we were kids." Speaking softly, Jeremiah took a step closer.

"I—I haven't?" Was he going to try to steal another? Just in case, she kept her chin tilted upward to give him easy access.

He reached forward, and Emily's eyes shut as though of their own accord. Her mind conjured up the memory of his palm against her cheek just before he had leaned in and kissed her all those years ago.

"Here you go," he said.

When no kiss was forthcoming, Emily's eyes shot open. She stared into Jeremiah's amused face.

"This was in your hair."

Emily looked dumbly at the loose thread he held between his thumb and forefinger. Then clarity broke through her romance-filled imagination. She brushed the thread from his fingers and scowled, planting her hands firmly on her hips.

"If you aren't going to work for me, then what do you intend to do?"

All amusement left Jeremiah's face, and a flush deepened

his tan. He turned away and opened the ledger, mumbling.

Emily gasped. "It sounded like you said opening your own store. Is that what you said?" Horror of horrors, Jeremy wouldn't do that to her, would he?

He turned to her slowly, gentleness shining in his soft brown eyes. "Harper has grown so much in the last few years, it can easily support two mercantiles. Don't you think?"

"I can't believe you're going into business against me, Jeremy. Of all the spiteful, mean things to do." She glared at him, fighting to keep her tears at bay. "I would never have thought it of you."

"Don't take it so personally. This is about my need to run my own business." His expression grew distant. "I would have done it years ago, but I thought I'd someday buy out Tucker."

"I see. You wouldn't compete against Mr. Tucker, but you have no problem trying to force me out of business."

"It's not like that, Emily." He frowned. "And don't you think you're overreacting just a bit?"

"Overreacting? No, I don't." She grabbed her bonnet from the peg behind the counter and stomped toward the door. "I think you're a low-down, sneaky. . .business stealer; and I don't want to be in the same room with you. Lock up when you leave, please."

Emily yanked the door shut and hurried down the stairs. She stopped short and gasped when she reached the bottom step. Turning, she made her way back to the door. Jeremiah glanced up as the bell dinged her entrance.

"Forget something?" he asked cooly.

"Y–you're still going to stay on until the end of the month, right?"

An indulgent smile lifted the corners of his lips, and the hard glint in his eyes softened. "I won't leave until I'm sure you know everything necessary to run this place."

Relief coursed through Emily, weakening her knees. *Thank You, God, that he isn't abandoning me.*

He glanced at her cautiously, curiously.

Still stinging from the revelation of Jeremiah's plans, Emily wasn't ready to make up with her old school chum. She sniffed. "Well, good. It's nice to see you've retained some semblance of chivalry."

Jeremiah chortled.

"What's so funny?" Emily demanded.

"I thought you 'equal suffrage' women were opposed to chivalry."

Emily's brow furrowed. "That shows how much you know about our cause! We're simply tired of being treated like slaves and. . .and being kicked around like starving, stray dogs, Jeremiah Daniels."

His eyes twinkled as his gaze traveled over her. "One look at you and anyone could tell you've certainly been deprived of nourishment and kicked around."

Heat rose to Emily's cheeks. Her eyes grew wide, and suddenly she became conscious of her plump hips and thick waist. She stared, so shocked by his reference to her figure, that she couldn't even muster enough anger to retort. "Why, Jeremiah. . . ," she finally squeaked. Then, unable to continue, she spun around and left before she made a spectacle of herself by weeping out her humiliation right there in the mercantile.

Tears stung Emily's eyes as she stomped toward the livery to pick up her horse and buggy. No wonder Jeremiah had never looked at her twice. He thought she was too fat! Emily sighed. She had to admit she had filled out quite a bit since graduating from the small-town school seven years earlier.

Still, that was the least of her worries right now. More pressing was the issue of Emily's Place. How could she run the store alone? She had to find a way to change Jeremiah's mind.

It had never even occurred to her that he wouldn't want to stay and run the mercantile. He had worked for Mr. Tucker since his schooldays when he stocked and dusted shelves after school and on Saturdays. Jeremiah working somewhere else just didn't seem right. He belonged with the mercantile. Besides, Emily needed him.

"Yoohoo, Emily!"

Emily turned at the sound of Mrs. Thomas's singsong voice. The older woman pulled her buggy beside the boardwalk. Forcing a cheery smile, Emily tried to push away her troubling thoughts of Jeremiah. "Good afternoon, Mrs. Thomas."

"Hello, Dear. You haven't forgotten tonight's meeting, have you?"

"No, Ma'am." As if she could forget that tonight she had to stand in front of a crowd of women and give a speech. When she'd signed on, she never intended to be a vocal force in the group, only a supporter and maybe hold up an occasional sign demanding the right to vote. She'd never counted on the knee-knocking experience she was in for this evening.

"We're all very excited to have Harper's newest woman entrepreneur in our little group of soldiers." The older woman flashed a wide grin. "Amelia Bell actually gained permission to cover the meeting for her pa's newspaper. What do you think of that? You're already making a difference for the women of this town."

Emily flushed with pleasure at the praise. "I'm glad I can help the cause, Mrs. Thomas."

"It's too bad we can't convince your mother to join. Cassidy St. John would be a mighty shot in the arm for the Kansas Equal Suffrage Association."

"I—I could speak to her, if you'd like."

Mrs. Thomas beamed as though Emily had made the most brilliant of statements. "Lovely! Just lovely! I knew you would be an amazing asset to our endeavor."

"Thank you, Ma'am."

Mrs. Thomas gave a swift nod. "I must be going. I have a million things to do before the meeting tonight." She suddenly leaned toward Emily. "Oh, and Dear, I've been informed that the League of Christian Women intends to protest our cause from right outside the door. But don't let that discourage you. Hold your head high, and remember, God is on the side of right. And we, my dear, are right!" She raised her fist in the air. "Votes for women."

Emily returned the salute. "Votes for women," she echoed weakly, watching the matron drive away at breakneck speed.

Turning back toward the livery, she stiffened her spine and lifted her chin. She was Emily St. John, a woman of independent means. She didn't need a man, least of all Jeremiah Daniels, to make her business a success. She'd show him. Her store would outsell his by a mile. Then the good folks of Harper, Kansas, would see that she was just as special as the rest of the St. Johns, even if she wasn't smart like Sam or funny like Luke and Jack, or clever like Will, or beautiful like the girls. She would do this on her own, and Emily's Place would be the talk of the town.

❧

Jeremiah watched Emily through the store window until she stepped into the livery stable and out of his view. What had he said to upset her so? Mulling over the conversation, he suddenly groaned. He'd made reference to her figure. Wasn't his ma always lamenting her own plumpness? How could he have been dumb enough to practically come out and tell Emily she looked fat? Inwardly he kicked himself. He certainly hadn't meant to imply she wasn't attractive because of a little plumpness—truth be told, he found her round cheeks most becoming. And he'd had to force himself to look away from her womanly curves more than once since she'd been coming to the store every day. Even now, the memory of catching her in his arms quickened his pulse.

He'd have to apologize for hurting her feelings, but for now he couldn't get sidetracked by the only girl he'd ever had any desire to court. If he allowed his feelings for her to rule him, he'd stay here and make her business a success and forget about his own dreams—dreams that for a brief moment appeared to be coming true.

Last month he'd put away the last of the money needed to make Tucker a fair offer on the store. He was on the verge of asking Emily if he could call on her when she received the letter about her inheritance.

He scowled and turned his attention back to the ledger. His ledger. Or it should have been. After his years of working for Mr. Tucker, he couldn't believe Emily would just waltz in and take over. Lock, stock, and barrel. She knew—everyone knew—how much he'd always counted on buying this place from Tucker. She had to have known. And she had the nerve to call him a business stealer.

He glanced around the familiar room. If he closed his eyes, he could still see every single inch of the place, from the pickle barrel in front of the counter to the ever-present display of Healy's Magic Elixir, to the newly arrived stack of dime novels—rubbish to be sure, but amazingly fast sellers.

Since Tucker's marriage to Emily's granny, Jeremiah had pretty much run the place on his own. Like most newly married men, Tucker couldn't focus on much but the love of his life and could rarely be bothered with store business. And that suited Jeremiah perfectly fine.

He paid a neighboring boy a small sum to help him work the farm, and he had been able to save most of his wages from the store for the past several years. Then Emily had swooped down and pulled the rug right out from under him before he could make an offer on the place.

A fire of resentment burned inside of him at the unfairness of it all. He glanced across the street to the empty lot and saw what it would become. A bigger store than this one with Jeremiah's Mercantile written in large letters above the door. He might even get one of those fake storefronts he'd seen in Abilene. Something fancy maybe. Eye catching. Something to make folks pass Emily's Place right up and head for Jeremiah's instead.

The look of fear on Emily's face and her pleading tone came back to his mind, bringing with it a prick of guilt. Hopefully, his words to her would prove true and Harper could support two stores, but if not. . .

He hated to put her out of business, but she was a St. John, after all. Her store was another hobby. Like teaching school had been. Okay, so maybe she had lasted as teacher longer than he'd expected her to, but everyone knew she'd never liked the position. And if her pa hadn't been on the town council and county board for the past twenty years, she probably wouldn't have gotten the position in the first place. He knew Emily. She didn't like not getting her way. But he could handle himself just fine. Only he'd better avoid those enormous green eyes of hers or they'd be his undoing.

three

Emily focused her attention on transferring thick slices of ham from the skillet to a platter. She cut a glance to her ma and drew a deep, shaky breath before resuming her plea. "So, I hoped you might consider coming?"

"My goodness, Emily. Why didn't you tell us sooner about your speech tonight?" Cassidy St. John pushed back a loose strand of wayward, graying hair and leveled her gaze at Emily.

Emily shrugged and looked away. "I don't know. I didn't want you to feel compelled to come if you don't want to. You're not exactly supportive of the cause."

Ma moved toward the kitchen door with a basket of biscuits. She smiled over her shoulder. "And what's different now? Let me guess: Mrs. Thomas asked you to try to get me involved?"

Emily followed, carrying the platter of meat. "Something like that." There was no point in trying to deny it. Mrs. Thomas had been plaguing Ma for months with literature and suggestions that she at least "give the movement a try." Ma politely refused each time, and she had not been happy when Emily announced her intention to join the cause. *But after all*, Emily thought, *I'm a grown woman of twenty-five and own a business.*

Shaking her head in disgust, Ma pushed open the kitchen door with her elbow. "That woman. She never gives up!"

"Who never gives up?" Pa asked from his place at the head of the table.

"Mrs. Thomas. She asked Emily to invite me to the Equal Suffrage Association meeting tonight."

"You're not going, are you?" Pa winked at Emily and slid

his arm about Ma's thickening waist as she set the basket of biscuits in front of him. "One independent woman in this family is enough. I prefer my woman at home where she can keep an eye on me."

"Oh, you. Keeping an eye on you is a full-time job in itself. I don't have time to fight for a woman's right to vote." Ma stood still for a moment, allowing him the embrace, then she dropped an affectionate kiss on the top of his head and walked to her chair at the other end of the table.

Will and Jack, the only two boys still living at home, snickered with their pa. Will elbowed his older brother. "What do you think, Jack? Can't you just see our ma carrying a banner and marching down Main Street?" He held up an imaginary sign. "Votes for women!" he said in a forced, high-pitched tone.

Emily's defenses rose. Why did they always have to dismiss the cause as though it were mere women's foolishness?

"You boys hush up," Ma admonished, then focused her attention on Pa. "Dell, Darling, Emily feels very strongly about women gaining the right to vote. I believe we should both go and support her."

"You expect me to go to a women's rights rally?" he asked in mock horror, but he added with a grin, "I'm afraid my stump's paining me too much to sit through a meeting tonight."

Despite her cause being put up for public ridicule, Emily bit back a giggle. Since losing his leg several years ago after a bull attack, Pa had, on occasion, used the misfortune to gain an advantage.

Only this time it appeared Ma was having none of it. Her brow rose, and she eyed him sternly. "Hogwash. If I can go and put up with Mrs. Thomas, you can sit for an hour or two. Besides, our own daughter is giving a speech."

"It's all right, Ma." Emily set the platter none too gently onto the wooden table and flounced to her own chair. "You needn't bother yourselves on my account. I am perfectly capable of attending alone."

"Let's say grace, please, before the meal gets cold." Ma folded her plump hands and gave a pointed glance to each family member seated at the table. "We'll discuss this matter while we eat."

After Pa said the blessing, he reached out and patted Emily's hand. Emily felt the tears rise and sting her eyes at his gentle condescension. "Now, Sweetheart. Don't get upset. We'll go to your meeting."

Twenty-two-year-old Jack coughed loudly. Will pounded him on the back. Once he regained his composure, Jack sent Pa an incredulous look over the rim of his milk glass as he washed down his bite. "You mean you're actually going?"

"Of course. Didn't you hear your ma? Emily's giving a speech. I wouldn't miss it for anything."

Clearly unmoved by the strong show of family support, Jack gave a deep scowl and pressed his side of the issue. "But we won't be able to hold up our heads in decent company if she gets up on the platform and starts shouting about equality and the right to vote. Don't let her do it, Pa."

"That's right," Will echoed. "What kind of example is that setting for the other girls?" He cast a pointed glance at his twin sister, Hope, and their baby sister, thirteen-year-old Cat.

Hope sniffed and raised her chin slightly. "As if I'd set foot in a meeting for that disgraceful movement. I have enough on my mind lately, planning my wedding. What do I care about women who wear bloomers and smoke cigars?"

A gasp escaped Cat's rosebud mouth, commanding attention from her family.

"What's wrong, Sugarbaby?" Emily asked, frowning.

"I can't believe Hope doesn't support votes for women. And besides, most of the women don't smoke anyway, do they, Emily?" Her wide blue eyes begged Emily to dispel the awful rumor.

"Of course not." Emily settled an affectionate smile on her baby sister—clearly the beauty in a family of attractive girls and handsome boys. Her hair, the color of spun gold, fell in ringlets down her back. "Do I?" Emily asked the angelic-looking child.

A grin curved Cat's lips. "I should think not!"

"I don't see why girls think they have a right to vote, anyway," Will said with the wisdom only a seventeen year old could muster. "Personally, I wouldn't want to live in a country where my president was decided by a woman."

Although she knew better than to have this debate, Emily couldn't help defending her newfound cause. "It's about more than the right to vote," she retorted. "It's equal humanity we want. Women worked just as hard as men to settle this land. Since the end of the war, we have educated the young men who fill the voting booths all across this country; and yet if I were to step foot into one of those very booths and try to cast my vote, I would be arrested. Why shouldn't we have a say in the way things are run?"

Will regarded her smugly. "The declaration says all men were created equal. Not women."

"And who taught you that?" Emily raised her brow.

Ma and Pa each let out a chuckle.

Will's face reddened considerably. He stuffed a forkful of ham into his mouth.

Emily gave him a self-satisfied smirk. "I, a lowly woman, taught you everything you know about our government."

"Those women are disgraceful," he said, obviously undaunted. "And whether most women in the group smoke or not, I saw Mrs. Krenshaw smoking a cigar the other day. And she's taken to wearing trousers and cut her hair off short like a man's. Poor Mr. Krenshaw. I wouldn't stand for it, if I were him."

"Now, Will. You know better than to judge a person by outward appearance," Ma admonished.

"Sorry," he muttered and shoveled another bite into his mouth.

Ma scooped potatoes onto her plate, then paused with the spoon still in hand. "Mr. Krenshaw seems to be holding his own. He goes with Mrs. Krenshaw to the meetings."

Will snorted. "She probably threatens him with a good lashing if he doesn't."

"Honestly." Ma shook her head. "Hush and eat your supper."

"And women say they're treated like an inferior class." Will elbowed Jack.

"Yeah, Ma runs this family with an iron hand."

"You two. . ." Ma blushed and smiled affectionately at her sons, then turned to Emily. "What are you going to wear to the meeting, Honey?"

"Actually. . ." Emily's gaze darted around the table. She had wanted to ask Ma in private. She cleared her throat. "I hoped you'd lend me your old bloomer outfit."

"My what?"

"You know. The bloomer outfit you wore on the trip from Missouri. Way back when you first married Pa."

"Emily St. John, that's ancient. I wouldn't know where to begin looking for it. Why on earth would you want to wear something so outdated, anyway?"

"They've become quite fashionable again. Especially among suffragettes, Mama," Cat piped in. "I planned to ask for one myself, since I'm joining Emily's group as soon as I'm old enough."

Emily smiled at the youngest member of the family. "Hopefully, by that time we'll have gained our right to vote, Sugarbaby; but if not, you'll be a welcome addition to our cause."

"You can always ask Laney if she'll loan you a pair of her trousers, Em," Hope said, disdain thick in her already husky voice. "She hardly ever wears them anymore except when she's working the cattle."

Emily scowled at her sister. Like she'd be able to fit one leg inside Laney's tiny jeans. "I don't want to wear men's clothing.

Just comfortable women's clothing. Bloomer outfits are still made for women, even if they are bloomers."

"I'm afraid you'll just have to wear a dress tonight," Ma said. "But we'll visit Laney and have a bloomer outfit made for you very soon."

"And me?" Cat asked.

"You'll have to take that up with your pa."

Cat turned her wide, pleading eyes upon Pa. "Please?"

Shaking his head, Pa admitted his defeat with an indulgent smile. "I suppose so. But you are only allowed to wear it at home and on picnics. Is that understood?"

Her hopeful expression dropped, but Cat nevertheless nodded, bouncing her curls around her shoulders. "Yes, Sir."

"What is your speech going to be about, Emily?"

Staring dumbly at Ma, Emily felt the heavy weight on her shoulders of what she was going to do. How in the world could she stand up in front of those women and speak? Suddenly ill, she pushed back her plate. "I'm sorry, Ma. M—may I be excused?"

"Of course. Are you all right, Em?"

Emily nodded and fled the room just as her stomach protested her supper. Fighting nausea, she prayed. *Please, Lord. Help me get through tonight.* Oh, why had she ever agreed to speak about women having the right to their own businesses?

The only reason she had even bought Tucker's in the first place was so she could be near Jeremy every day. It had only become a matter of independence after Mrs. Thomas had made an issue of it.

It felt good to do something no one else in her accomplished family had ever done. She wanted to make a difference, wanted to be recognized as more than the girl Cassidy brought with her when she moved to Kansas to marry Dell St. John.

Emily wondered, as she had many times since receiving her

inheritance from her maternal grandmother, what it might have been like if her real ma and pa hadn't died, leaving her to be raised by her aunt Cassidy. Not that she didn't love Cassidy and Dell as though they were truly her parents. But in a family where everyone was beautiful and accomplished, it was difficult to be ordinary.

≈

"And to think, at one time I had hoped you'd marry that Emily St. John. Thank the merciful Lord in heaven He didn't see fit to answer my prayer on that one."

Jeremiah cut a sideways glance at his mother, who sat next to him on the wagon seat. He, too, had been surprised to learn of Emily's involvement with the suffrage movement, but nowhere near as upset as his poor mother. It came as quite a blow for her to discover Emily wasn't fit to be the mother of her future grandchildren, after all.

"Her ma and pa must be absolutely mortified at her disgraceful behavior."

"Disgraceful?" Jeremiah couldn't keep the defender in him from rising. "All she's doing is giving a speech about being a woman in business. Personally, I don't see why she shouldn't."

From the corner of his eye, Jeremiah saw his mother's cheeks puff out in indignation. "That girl has no business even owning that store. Everyone knows it was rightfully yours, and she stole it right out from under you. Then adding insult to injury, she joins those radicals. Well, I hope you put her out of business right quick."

"A Christian attitude, to be sure."

"Oh, fiddlesticks. We'll be doing her a favor by putting her out of business. Then she can concentrate on finding a husband, as God intended."

"I see. You're watching out for her soul."

"Exactly," Ma said, obviously missing the sarcasm in Jeremiah's tone. "My league and I certainly have no intention of patronizing her store once yours is opened. Of course, we have no choice until then."

"Of course," Jeremiah said wryly. "Otherwise, where would you buy those dime novels?"

"Don't be smart. You're still not too big for me to turn over my knee."

Jeremiah pulled on the reins, halting the horses in the yard before the meeting hall. Already most of the League of Christian Women had gathered to protest the meeting inside, and his mother was chomping at the bit to join them. He hopped down and offered her his assistance.

"You stay put until I'm ready to leave," she commanded. "I don't want to have to wait on you."

"Yes, Ma." He grinned. Ma had the patience of a hungry puppy. He couldn't resist teasing her. "I'm just going to head to the dance hall for awhile. You let me know when you're ready to go."

Her eyes twinkled in the glow of the moon. She gave him a whack on the arm. "You go anywhere near that evil place, and I'll whip the hide off you."

Bending, he kissed her on the cheek. "Go ahead and protest women's rights to your heart's content, and I'll be here waiting for you when you lose your voice and have no choice but to go home."

"Oh, you. You could come with me. I see little Hope St. John joining in the protest."

"Sorry, Ma. She's spoken for. Besides, I think she's headed away from the meeting, toward the Evans's place. She must have come into town with Emily's folks."

Ma's expression dropped. "What a pity."

A chuckle rose inside of Jeremiah. "One St. John girl is as good as another? How about I wait a few more years and try to woo little Cat?"

"You're being smart again." With that she sniffed and headed toward the group of protesters.

Jeremiah turned back to the wagon, wondering what in the

world he was going to do for the next two hours. Tempted to sneak inside so he could hear Emily's speech, he glanced at the convoluted entrance to the meeting hall. There was no way he could sneak past Ma, and she'd be humiliated if he showed a hint of support for the suffragettes.

With a sigh, he climbed back into the wagon seat, stretched out his legs, and folded his arms across his chest. Shutting his eyes, he settled in for a nice long wait.

"Psst."

His eyes shot open and he sat straight up. He twisted, looking from one side of the wagon to the other, trying to locate the source of the whisper. When his search yielded no answers, he frowned and shivered, though the midsummer breeze blew warm against his neck. "Who's there?"

"It's me, Emily."

Turning, he spied her lying flat in the back of his wagon. "What are you doing?"

"Please, Jeremy," she pleaded, her voice trembling. "For mercy's sake, hurry and get me out of here before they find me."

four

A quarter mile from town, Jeremiah halted the horses. Emily sat up in the back of the wagon, breathing a relieved sigh to be away from the meeting. "I don't know how to thank you, Jeremy."

"Hang on." Jeremiah wrapped the reins around the brake and climbed down. He walked to the back of the wagon and hopped onto the tailboard. "Now, you want to tell me what this is all about?" He scooted in, swung his legs up, and rested his back against the side of the wagon, facing her.

Emily glanced down at her fingers. "All those women. Inside the building, they were chanting about women's rights. And outside. . ." She shuddered. "A mob. Just like during the French Revolution. I thought my head was going to roll any second."

Jeremy gave a deep chuckle. "With my ma leading the angry pack."

"That's right. She's head of the League of Christian Women. I forgot." It certainly wouldn't do for Emily to spout off anything unflattering about the League. She refused to antagonize Jeremiah before she convinced him to give up his silly idea of building his own store. She had to make him see that teaming up would be more profitable for them both than pitting two stores against each other.

"How did you sneak out without being seen?"

"I told Mrs. Thomas I had to visit the. . ." Emily felt the heat rush to her face.

Thankfully, Jeremiah nodded understandingly. "Clever ploy."

Emily opened her mouth to set him straight, then changed

her mind. Better to let him think she'd told a bold-faced lie than to admit she'd actually made a dash for the privy as her stomach churned at the thought of facing those women. That would be too humiliating.

"What else was I to do?"

He shrugged. "You could have stayed and given your speech."

Emily's temper flared. "With all that racket going on outside from your ma and her cronies? I was nervous enough as it was."

"If you're going to be a pioneer, you have to expect some opposition."

The anger sifted from her as she mulled over his words. "Honestly. I don't want to be a pioneer. I just want. . ."

What did she want? Certainly not to march through town shouting for rights. Not to go to her store every day and haggle over prices or stock shelves.

"Do you even know what you want, Emily?" Jeremiah's tone was gentle, without any condemnation. "Why did you buy Tucker's? You could have taken the money or part of the money you inherited and traveled to England or back East. You could have set yourself up in a nice little house in town and lived comfortably on your teaching salary. Why the mercantile?"

A heavy sigh escaped her lips. "I don't know. After you mentioned that Tuck was selling and I got news of my inheritance, it just seemed like the right thing to do. I never thought you might not stay and run it. That was the sole reason for. . ."

"The sole reason for what? What do you mean?"

"Oh, nothing. I just wanted to buy it and Tucker wanted to sell. So that's that."

"All right. That explains the store—somewhat. What about this Kansas Equal Suffrage—"

"Don't call it nonsense," Emily cut in.

"I wasn't going to," he retorted. "Do you really feel that strongly about women having the right to vote?"

Resting the back of her head against the side of the wagon, Emily stared into the glorious, star-dotted expanse above. "Oh, Jeremy. I never thought much about it until I heard Mrs. Thomas speak. But now. . ." How did she explain that she wanted respect, the kind of respect that only came with finding your own place in the world? Having a voice that counted for something? "I believe women should have the same civil liberties men enjoy. Aren't we citizens of the United States?"

"I see your point."

"Do you?" Emily had expected an argument similar to the constant berating she received from her brothers.

"Of course. I see no reason you shouldn't be allowed to cast your vote."

Affection swelled Emily's chest. Jeremiah Daniels was a rare man indeed. Of course, she'd always known that.

"Just don't take to chawing and spitting." He grinned, and Emily thought her heart might stop from the pure joy of being the recipient of such a smile.

"Don't worry about that," she replied, returning his smile. "Besides, they'll probably kick me out of the association when they realize I'm not coming back. I figure I have about another hour before they announce me and realize I hightailed it out of there." Emily's heart sank at the thought. Would she ever succeed at anything?

Jeremiah slapped his thigh and hopped from the wagon. "I have an idea. How about you go back and give your speech?"

Emily gasped. "I can't go back now! How would it look?"

"It would look a whole lot better than running away like a coward. Stay and face it, Em. If you don't want to be in the movement after tonight, then don't be. But at least give yourself the opportunity to be a success. Who knows? Your speech may be the one that encourages some destitute widow to start selling baked goods from her home. And what if it turned into a thriving business and she opened her own bakery right here in Harper?" He reached across the wagon and gripped her hand. "You're the only woman in town who owns a business. Even Laney gave up sewing for Tucker when she and Luke made a go of the Double L ranch. You have to set a good example for the women who need to be independent. Every unmarried woman has to be able to take care of herself. You can show them they don't need to worry if they can't find a husband. It's possible for a woman to go it alone if she needs to."

Emily gasped. Jeremiah didn't think she could find a husband? Is that why he was being so nice to her? Pity! She focused her gaze on him, hoping the full moon shining across the back of the wagon afforded enough light for him to catch the full force of her glare. "You're right. I do need to show the unmarried women just how wonderful it is not to be encumbered with a tyrannical man who only wants a woman to cook and clean and raise a passel of babies. I—I thank you kindly, Jeremiah Daniels, for setting my thinking straight. Only a foolish woman would want to marry when she can have a business instead. Please return me to the meeting hall so I can give my speech."

❧

Confused, Jeremiah glanced at Emily, who sat ramrod straight and completely silent in the seat next to him. Well, she wasn't exactly sitting next to him. Rather, she sat as close to the edge as she could manage without tumbling to the ground. As it was, he found himself maneuvering the horses with added care so as not to hit a pothole and bounce her from the seat.

He turned his attention back to the road, puzzling over the sudden change in her demeanor. He'd been encouraged by their discussion until the bit about women in business. Was it possible she didn't want other women to take away from her position as the only businesswoman in Harper? He dismissed the thought as absurd. Emily wasn't petty. Prickly, at times, yes. But not petty.

When the lamplights of Harper came into view, he'd had all he could take of her silence. "All right, Emily. Enough is enough. Are you going to tell me what I said that offended you all of a sudden?"

Emily pressed her lips together and jerked her chin upward.

"Fine." Jeremiah pulled on the reins, stopping the horses in the middle of the road. "We're not going another foot without an explanation."

"I'll walk, then." Emily started to climb down; as she did, her dress caught beneath her heel, making her stumble.

Jeremiah reached across the seat and grabbed her arm to steady her.

"Don't you dare manhandle me, Jeremiah Daniels! I may not have a man of my own, but I have a pa and four huge brothers."

With a scowl, Jeremiah turned her loose, but only after assuring himself she wouldn't tumble headlong to the damp ground. "I was only—"

"So you see, even if I can't find a husband, I'll always have someone to protect me!"

A frown creased Jeremiah's brow. What was she talking about. . .husbands and protection? Protection from him? Then understanding dawned, and he couldn't help but laugh. "Oh, you thought I meant you couldn't find a husband."

"Well, that was your allusion, wasn't it? I'm glad you think it's so funny."

Jeremiah's pulse picked up, and all thoughts of teasing fled as he observed her lip tremble. He reached over and, at the risk of being accused of manhandling again, he took her soft hand and held it. "Emily, I didn't mean you couldn't find a man. I don't figure you want one, or you'd have had some lucky fellow at the altar years ago."

He swallowed past a lump in his throat as she turned her wide, tear-pooled eyes upon him.

"Really?"

"Of course," he said, his voice suddenly raspy. "I only meant for women who are alone, whether by choice or necessity, you're a good one for them to look up to."

Her lips curved into a beautiful smile. She placed her free hand over their clasped hands. "Thank you, Jeremy. I apologize for the misunderstanding."

"I'm the one who should apologize. I seem to make a habit of saying the wrong thing."

"We'll pretend it never happened."

As much as he hated to, Jeremiah slipped his hand free and gathered up the reins once more. "I'd best get you back so you can give your speech."

Emily cleared her throat, then turned to him suddenly. "You know, I don't believe in the cause to the exclusion of marriage and family. I—It's just that the right man has never asked."

Another man might have considered her statement an opening, an offer that she might not reject a proposal or at least the request to court her properly; but Jeremiah knew he was in no position to marry a girl like Emily. Besides, she was the daughter of the most successful rancher in three counties. While he, on the other hand, would always be the grubby little boy who stole sourballs from Tucker's store.

Jeremiah sighed. Perhaps if his business proved successful. Maybe then he'd be good enough for Emily. A month ago, he would have jumped on her statement like a fish on a worm. Now that she'd bought the mercantile, he had no choice but to wait and see how his new store fared in the scheme of things before he'd be in a position to consider courting.

"I'm sure when that lucky man comes along, he'll be praising God that you're not opposed to marrying and settling down."

"Yes," she replied flatly. "I'm sure you're right."

The remainder of the trip into town was uncomfortably silent. Jeremiah knew better than to try to explain. It would only make things worse.

❧

Emily lay in her bed, mulling over the events of the evening.

Her speech had gone off without a hitch; and when she slipped back inside, it appeared no one had even noticed she'd been gone. Afterwards, ladies of all ages had surrounded her, flattering her, thanking her for giving their cause another voice in the community.

Emily had the uncomfortable feeling that many of the more mature members of the group only welcomed her in an effort to woo Ma to the association. Mrs. Thomas fawned all over poor Ma the minute she stepped in the door. Like most women in love, Ma was content to take care of Pa and the family. While she might believe in the cause of women's rights, she certainly wouldn't make a habit of leaving home to attend rallies and marches. And she had told Mrs. Thomas so, in no uncertain terms.

Rolling onto her back, Emily stared at the moonlit ceiling. The time she'd spent with Jeremiah would remain imprinted on her heart forever—partly a sweet memory and partly bitter.

If only she hadn't told him she'd like to get married, should the right man ask her! She groaned, feeling ill from the memory of her brazen hinting. What must he think of her now? He'd been gracious, but clearly not tempted to take her up on her invitation.

Despite her glum musings, a grin tipped the corners of her lips at the thought of Jeremiah sneaking into the meeting hall to hear her speech. He'd smiled broadly at her and was the first to his feet, leading the ovation as she said the words, "So, let us rise up and attend our own businesses. If we can run our homes and raise good, Christian children who contribute to the betterment of society, why can't we run profitable businesses, void of the management of men? Who is to say that we can't remain fine, upstanding citizens of the community without spot or blemish to tarnish our reputations?"

With a start, Emily sat up in bed. Perhaps she didn't need Jeremiah to manage Emily's Place at all! What if she could attend her own business and really make it a success?

What if she went so far as to move into Tucker's old rooms above the store? A bubble of excitement rose inside her. She would truly be on her own. The bubble deflated in an instant of new thought. What if Jeremiah decided to court her? He couldn't very well do that if she were living alone.

Releasing a sigh, Emily flopped back onto her feather pillow. Jeremiah had made it abundantly clear, despite her unabashed hinting, that he wasn't interested in courting her anyway, so what was the point in waiting around?

For the rest of the night, her mind whirled with activity as she organized her thoughts into what it would take to set up housekeeping for herself. Now, how would she convince Ma and Pa it was a good idea?

Surprisingly, she received minimal argument from her parents; and within the week, Emily found herself on her own in every sense of the word.

As she lay in her bed the first night away from home, listening to the lonely silence of her own little three-room home above the mercantile, she couldn't keep the tears at bay. Suddenly, all she wanted was a little home of her own and a man to take care of her and give her a houseful of children.

Independence certainly wasn't all it was cracked up to be, and Emily knew she'd give it up in a heartbeat. . .if only the right man would ask her to.

five

Emily planted her chin in her palm and watched the influx of customers at the newly opened Jeremiah's Mercantile across the street.

She'd watched daily for the past two months as the store was built frame by frame, nail by nail—and she'd prayed for a miracle. When no divine intervention seemed likely, however, she'd resigned herself to the competition. Still, with dread, she had anticipated this day. And now the big opening was upon her.

Emily scowled at her empty store. Honestly, the lack of loyalty present in her customers was nothing less than shameful. No one seemed the least bit concerned about how she might feel as they happily entered the enemy's camp and came out with their ill-gotten goods.

Well, she, for one, was not about to let it bother her. Once folks realized that she had better prices and better-quality goods, they'd be back. Only—she stomped her foot—how much was Jeremiah charging, anyway? She couldn't very well go over and find out. And if she sent one of her family members, Jeremiah would know they were nothing more than spies.

It wasn't fair. He knew every single item she had for sale, and he knew exactly how much she charged.

Suddenly, a huge, marvelous idea entered her mind. Joy bubbled in her soul. She would mark prices down and undersell Jeremiah by a mile. A quick glance around brought a new worry. Only, how would she get the word out?

She planted her hands on her hips and released a quick breath as she thought. *The Harper Herald!* With a grin, she closed up the empty store and headed down the sidewalk to the paper office. Amelia Bell, the owner's daughter, met her at the door and ushered her inside. "What can I do for you, Emily?"

"I need to place an ad in the newspaper."

Amelia grabbed a pencil and walked around the counter. "What kind of an ad?"

"Well, I'm having a sale on certain items in the store, and I. . .um. . .need to let folks know about it."

"That's a wonderful idea! The perfect way to steal back your customers."

"I'm not trying to. . ." Oh, what was the point? Of course she was trying to lure folks back to her store.

A look of expectancy crossed Amelia's features. "What items?"

Emily drew in her lip. "I'm not sure. I hadn't thought of it." She shot her gaze to Amelia. "What do you suggest?"

The other woman tapped her ink-stained fingers on the counter, staring as though she were deep in thought. Suddenly her eyes unclouded and she slapped the countertop. "I have it!"

Emily jumped at the sudden movement. "What?"

"You need to lower prices on items folks need for everyday. Not boot black or things like that. But things like flour, sugar, eggs, and beans."

"Why, I can't mark all those things down. I wouldn't make a cent! I might as well put up a sign that says, 'Come grab whatever you want. No charge.' "

"That'll bring all your customers back," Amelia said wryly. "All right. Pick two items."

"Flour and let's see. . .how about flannel? Mrs. Moody was just saying the other day the price of flannel is ridiculous and how was a body to afford to dress her men warmly through-out the winter? Yes, I think flour and flannel are good places to start." Emily grinned and repeated it. "It has a nice ring to it. The Flour and Flannel Sale. What do you think?"

A crescent grin spread across Amelia's mouth. "Catchy. We'll have folks flocking back to Emily's Place in no time— that'll be five cents to run the ad."

Envisioning a barren Jeremiah's Mercantile while folks made a virtual run on Emily's Place brought a smile to Emily's lips, and she gladly handed over the money.

Amelia leaned across the counter and grinned conspiratorially. "All right. Now that business is out of the way, guess who asked me to the harvest dance?"

Staring at the woman, who was commonly referred to as owl-faced—though Emily would never call her such—Emily felt her heart plummet. Amelia had been invited to the dance? By a man? Well, that pretty much secured Emily's fate as the only woman who would be escorted by her pa. She fought to squelch the tears burning just behind her eyes.

"Oh, don't look so horrified." Amelia glanced cautiously around, then apparently satisfied no one was listening, she whispered, "Clyde Hampton!"

"Oh, my!"

"Poor man. I suppose he must be desperate if he's asking me to the dance, when everyone knows how bossy and stubborn I am." She laughed. "I told him, sure I'd go with him, but not to even bother asking me to marry him because I wasn't ready to settle down and become a mother to five kids."

"Well, only two are still at home," Emily replied, inwardly smarting because Clyde hadn't asked her. Not that she wanted to go with the red-faced sheep farmer. And she'd never marry him in a hundred years. Still, if he asked Amelia. . .

"Two are more than enough to convince me not to marry a man. Anyway, he rescinded his offer." At that, Amelia flung back her head of chestnut hair and laughed so loud, Mr. Bell entered from the back room.

"What are you doing out here, Amelia? I'm not paying you to stand around and talk to your friends."

Emily knew Mr. Bell didn't approve of her association with

his only daughter. He'd been aloof with her ever since Amelia cast her lot with Emily and the rest of the suffragists.

"Sorry, Pa. Emily just came in to place an ad in the paper." She held up the nickel. "Bought and paid for—just the kind of customer you like."

He gave Emily a tight smile and nodded before heading back to his presses and inks.

Amelia watched until he disappeared, then she turned back to Emily. "Has anyone asked you yet?"

Yet? As if anyone would.

"No. But I always go with my pa and ma."

"I know. Because no one asks you," she said flatly. "And don't try to deny that you'd snatch up the offer to go with a decent man!"

Emily took no offense. Amelia was thoughtless and direct, but not intentionally unkind. And besides, no one ever asked the newspaperwoman to dances or out for buggy rides any more than they did Emily. "I suppose you're right. I would like to at least be asked to a dance."

Amelia stared reflectively, touching her pencil to her lip. "Too bad Jeremiah always has his ma to bring everywhere." She stared reflectively. "He'd ask you if he could, I bet."

Emily's heart leapt, though she knew Amelia was wrong. "I don't know what you mean. Besides, I told you, it's easier for Pa to pick me up—the dance is in our barn this year, after all. I have to be there early to help set up the refreshment table and such."

"Whatever you say." But her face showed obvious doubt. "I better get this back to Pa so we can get it printed. In the meantime, I'll pass along the word about your flour and flannel sale." She grinned. "It is rather catchy, isn't it?"

Emily couldn't help but return the smile. "Very catchy. I'll be going, then. Thank you, Amelia."

"Don't mention it. We women have to stick together, don't we?"

"Yes, I suppose we do."

Emily left the newspaper office with a light heart. She walked the few feet to her mercantile and paused to stare across at Jeremiah's before unlocking her own door. The parade of customers had died down, and she could see Jeremiah through the window, staring back at her. Her cheeks flamed, but she relaxed when he gave her an easy smile and waved. She returned his wave and smiled. After all, it wouldn't do for him to think she was holding a grudge.

As she stepped into Emily's Place, she pondered Amelia's words. Would Jeremiah have asked her to the dance if he weren't escorting his ma? She allowed herself a few minutes of dreamy "what ifs" until she heard the bell over the door ding. She looked up to find Clyde Hampton, hat in his hand, appearing very much as though he might want to ask a girl to a dance.

⁂

Jeremiah narrowed his gaze and shot a dark glance over the edge of his cup of apple cider while he sipped. The swirl of gaily colored gowns circling the dance floor made him dizzy as he tried to keep his eye on Emily and Clyde Hampton.

Emily was beautiful. . .dressed in a gown of emerald silk. Watching her made him ache to cut in on the dance. But he held his ground and gulped more of the cider.

"Thirsty, Jeremiah?" Amelia Bell's voice broke through his thoughts and drew his attention away from Emily and her dance partner.

"Hmm?"

"You must be awfully thirsty," she said, amusement thick in her voice and sparkling from enormous blue eyes peeking from behind her spectacles. "That's the third cup of cider you've gulped down during Emily's waltz with ol' Clyde. Why don't you just go cut in on him?"

Jeremiah scowled at the nosy little reporter. Why didn't she just go away and bother someone else?

She laughed and patted his shoulder. "Go on, Jeremiah. You know you can't bear having another man dancing with your girl. I think she'd be grateful. We all know what kind of a dancer Clyde is—bless his heart."

"What do you mean I can't bear the thought of anyone else dancing with my girl? Em's not my girl."

"Oh, really? Maybe not formally. . ."

Jeremiah opened his mouth to protest further, but Amelia held up her hand to silence him. "I'm a newspaperwoman. It's in my blood to sniff out the things that aren't so noticeable to anyone else. Stop pouting and go cut in on Clyde before he cripples poor Emily's toes." She grabbed the mug from his hands and gave him a little shove.

Jeremiah stumbled forward onto the dance floor. Couples swirled around him, throwing curious glances his way.

Locating Emily and Clyde, Jeremiah noted a wince on Emily's face. That did it. He was going to do something about that oaf trouncing all over her dainty little toes. He strode purposefully across the floor and tapped on Clyde's shoulder.

"May I?"

Reluctantly, Clyde stepped back. "Th—thank you for the dance, Miss Emily."

Emily's lips tilted in a kind smile. "My pleasure, Clyde. Thank you."

Once the niceties were out of the way and Clyde strode toward the refreshment table, Emily turned expectantly to Jeremiah. He gathered a breath and slid his hand along the silk at her waist, wishing he could pull her just a little closer like the married men held their wives.

"Are you enjoying the dance so far?" she asked him.

"I am now." He stared down into her eyes and smiled. No sense in pretending. "You look lovely."

Red blotches appeared on her neck and cheeks, but he didn't mind. No other woman in the room held a candle to Emily— red blotches or not.

"Thank you, Jeremy. You look very handsome as well."

His heart soared, and suddenly he was glad Ma had talked him into allowing her to make him a new tan jacket and trousers. His white shirt underneath was new as well, and he'd completed the look with a black string tie at his collar.

He stared down at her, wishing he could think of something else to say. For the sake of peace, they'd better steer clear of any conversation regarding the stores. But what did they talk about? They were enjoying the dance, and they'd discussed appearance.

He cleared his throat. "Nice night, isn't it?"

"Yes, it is. It's warm in here, though."

"It is. Let's go get some air."

"Miss Kitty had a new litter of kittens. Want to see them?"

Personally, Jeremiah didn't care where they went as long as they went together. "Sure."

"Let me run and grab my shawl and let Ma know where I'll be. I'll meet you out front in a few minutes."

Jeremiah smiled and took her elbow as he escorted her across the dance floor. She smiled as she left to find her shawl. He stepped outside into the cool autumn evening. Stuffing his hands into his pockets, he rocked back on his heels and stared into the starry sky.

He felt someone join him and glanced, expecting to find Emily. Instead, Harold Baxter stood next to him, smoke from a cigar swirling around him as he took a puff.

"Cigar?" Harold asked, reaching into his jacket.

"No thanks," Jeremiah replied, wishing the other man would take his revolting cigar and go someplace else. Harold had never been what he considered a friend. Even during their schooldays, they'd never had much in common.

"Saw you dancing with Emily." The man took another puff. "Good idea. Thought I might cut in until the two of you stopped dancing."

A surge of jealousy shot through Jeremiah. "That so?"

"Yep. You two courting?"

"No. Why?" Jeremiah asked, surprised at the hostility rising in him toward the other man.

"I was thinking of asking her if I could come calling."

"Is that right?"

Harold had known Emily forever. He had married young, but his bride had died giving birth to their only child two years after the wedding. Why hadn't he tried to court Emily before now if he was interested?

Why haven't you? The words taunted him as he considered the possibility of losing Emily forever. First Clyde, now Harold. Jeremiah could see he was going to have to do something—and quick.

Jeremiah cut a glance at Harold. "I planned to ask her tonight if I could come calling." And he was going to. He'd have preferred to wait until the store was holding its own a little better, but given the alternative, he wasn't willing to take the risk.

"Well, now. I guess we have ourselves a little problem, then." Harold sent him a good-natured grin.

"What sort of problem?" No one loved Emily the way he did, and Jeremiah just figured it was fitting for the other man to step aside and let him court her. If she was even willing.

"Miss Emily St. John has a lot more appeal now than she did before." He laughed. "And I don't just mean more to grab onto. But you already know that, don't you?"

Jeremiah frowned and balled his fists, ready to punch Harold if he was insulting Emily. "What sort of appeal are you referring to?" The other man could very well be innocent, in which case Jeremiah would forgive him. Emily had grown lovelier as she'd blossomed into womanhood, and the confidence she'd gained since owning the store was rather attractive as well. Perhaps those things appealed to Harold.

"Well, you know. The store. Any man would be daft not to try to marry her now—despite her figure."

Her figure? There was nothing wrong with Emily's figure—unless a man wanted a scrawny stick of a woman. As a matter of fact, Emily was the most becoming woman in town. This man didn't deserve her, and Jeremiah had no intention of allowing him the chance to break her heart by only marrying her for her business. He was just about to say so, when the other man spoke up. "Of course, there's that annoying suffragist matter. But I'll keep her too busy with our children to have time for that nonsense." He grinned and elbowed Jeremiah. "Know what I mean?"

Nearly choked with rage, Jeremiah faced him fully. "Listen here, Emily is spoken for. So you can get those ideas out of your head. And as far as the store is concerned, I've worked that place since I was twelve years old. If any man is going to run it for her, it'll be me. Not someone who doesn't know anything about storekeeping and might lose the whole thing."

Harold tossed his cigar on the ground and crushed it with his boot. "I guess we'll just have to see which of us she chooses." He extended his hand. "In the spirit of friendly competition for the fair Emily's hand in marriage and a nice profitable mercantile. . .may the best man win."

Jeremiah ignored the proffered hand and glanced away. Harold gave a short laugh. "Have it your own way."

Unable to speak for fear of saying too much, Jeremiah turned and strode toward the barn just as Amelia walked through the door on Clyde's arm. "Oh there you are, Jeremiah," she said. "My, it is hot inside. Emily asked me to let you know it's her turn to watch the refreshment table so she won't be able to show you the kittens after all. She didn't look too happy. As a matter of fact, she looked pretty pale and shaken."

He didn't blame her. Disappointment engulfed him as well. "Thanks for letting me know, Amelia."

"No problem. Clyde and I were just coming out for a breath of fresh air anyway. Weren't we, Clyde?" The sheep farmer glanced down at the little woman on his arm and grinned broadly.

"We sure were, Miss Amelia."

"Ta-ta, Jeremiah."

Jeremiah watched them go, wishing it were Emily on his arm. He shrugged and headed toward the barn. At least the cider was good.

❧

Emily stiffened her spine at the sight of Jeremiah heading toward the refreshment table. She'd traded shifts with Hope just for the excuse not to go outside with him, but it appeared she wouldn't be able to escape his presence after all.

If anyone is going to run Emily's store for her, it'll be me.

She'd been standing just behind the door when Harold Baxter began his insulting discourse. At first she'd thought Jeremiah might defend her, but that statement had been all she could take. Shaking inside from fury and heartbreak, Emily could barely bring herself to meet Jeremiah's gaze.

"I'm sorry we couldn't see the kittens," he said. "Another time maybe?"

Was this where he asked her if he could come courting?

"I don't know, Jeremiah. After all, I don't live here anymore." She filled a cup with cider and handed it to a thirsty child who smiled his thanks and bounded away.

"That's true, I suppose. Actually, what I meant was. . ." He cleared his throat. "Think I could have a cup of that cider?"

Grudgingly, Emily handed him some.

He gulped it down. "Thanks."

"What I actually meant was. . ."

"Evening, Miss Emily." Emily ignored Jeremiah's sudden scowl and forced herself to smile at Harold as he approached the refreshment table.

"Good evening, Harold. Would you like some cider?"

He leaned over the table and smiled what appeared to be an earnest smile, flashing beautifully white teeth. But Emily knew exactly what lurked behind his handsome face. A sneaky, low-down scoundrel out to take away her business. And she'd never forgive him for calling the cause nonsense.

Jeremiah shifted from one foot to the other. "Yes or no, Baxter."

"Excuse me?" The hostility in Harold's tone was unmistakable. Jeremiah stepped closer—an obvious challenge.

Emily had always dreamed of what it might be like for men to fight over her, but there was absolutely nothing flattering about having two men fighting over who got to steal her business out from under her while she stayed home and ironed his shirts!

"Do you want apple cider or not? Emily doesn't have all day while you think about it."

Harold turned his melting smile upon her. She might have found it tempting twenty minutes ago, but now she knew what he was about and she refused to be taken in by flashing white teeth and a handsome face.

"Did you make it, Emily?" he asked.

Barely able to remain civil, Emily dipped some of the sweet liquid for Harold. "No, I didn't. I am much too busy running my own store to bother with things like apple cider. Now if you two gentlemen will excuse me. I'm afraid I need to attend to others who might want refreshments."

"Of course." Harold took her hand and brought it to his lips. "May I have the honor of dancing the last waltz with you later?"

"Now, wait just a minute," Jeremiah broke in. "I already started to ask her for the last dance."

Emily glanced from one would-be husband to the next. "T–to tell you the truth," she said, fighting to keep back tears of humiliation, "I'm not feeling well. I believe I'll just go to the house now. You'll both have to find another dance partner for that waltz."

"All right," Harold said in that silky voice that Emily had

always found so appealing until now. "You go lie down. I'll talk to you soon." He strode away and caught hold of young Charity Smythe and whirled her onto the dance floor.

"Good night, Jeremiah," Emily said, hoping he'd take the hint. Instead, he frowned and swept his gaze over her face.

"You do look pale." Before she could move, Jeremiah brought his hand to her forehead. "You're warm too. Stay here. I'm going to go grab Sam and have him take a look at you."

"Oh, Jeremiah. Don't bother my brother. He's so busy doctoring this town, I haven't seen him having such a good time in so long."

Jeremiah hesitated. "All right, but promise me if you don't feel better tomorrow, you'll let him examine you."

Emily had to marvel at her change in perspective. If Jeremiah had shown this sort of concern before she learned the truth of his intentions, she might have honestly thought he cared. Now she realized he was only watching out for his interests. After all, if something were seriously wrong with her, she might not be around to marry him. Then Emily's Place would never be his. Fighting to hold back tears, Emily grabbed her shawl from the chair behind her and whipped it around her shoulders. "Will you watch the table for me until I can find Hope?"

"I'd rather walk you to the house. You shouldn't be alone." The concern edging his voice was nothing short of dramatic genius, and even Emily was almost fooled into thinking he might actually care. Then reality bit hard as Harold waltzed by and grinned at her, despite the beauty in his arms.

"I'll be fine. And I'd prefer to be alone, if you don't mind." Giving him no chance to further protest, Emily headed toward the door. Let him find his own replacement at the table. It served him right if he had to dip up apple cider for all the thirsty dancers. She fairly flew to the house, fighting to keep the tears at bay until she was alone. Once she reached her old bedroom and threw herself across the bed, full-blown sobs wracked her body.

Oh, Jeremiah, why?

God, why did You make me the way I am? Couldn't You have given me even one attribute that might cause a man to think me worth loving?

six

"How on earth could you run out of sugar a week before Christmas, Em?"

Standing before the shelf that only a month ago had been laden with bags of sugar, Emily stared at the barrenness. Her cheeks burned under Ma's incredulous gaze. Why, oh, why hadn't she listened when Jeremiah suggested she stock up?

Pride. That's all it had been. Stinking, sinful pride. And now she was paying the price for her stubbornness. But for mercy's sake, how could she possibly have known he was trying to help her, after he'd been underselling her for the past few weeks? She'd thought—and quite reasonably in her opinion—that he was simply trying to get her to overstock.

But, she couldn't admit that to Ma. "I can get a shipment the first week after Christmas," Emily said, knowing full well that wasn't soon enough.

Ma drew in her lower lip and shook her head in helpless appeal. "I'm sorry, Honey, but I'm afraid I have no choice but to buy what I need from Jeremiah. You know we'll have your brothers and sister and their families at the ranch on Christmas. We simply have to have plenty of goodies for the children."

Tears welled up in Emily's eyes, but she looked away. "I completely understand." She gave an airy laugh. "Jeremiah has plenty in stock. I saw him unloading an extra supply just the other day."

Obviously not a bit fooled by Emily's bravado, Ma gave her a sympathetic smile. "I promise not to spend so much as a penny over the cost of the sugar." She kissed Emily on the cheek and headed for the door.

"Give Jeremiah my best, and be sure to tell him I sent you over." It would do no good at all for him to imagine her sulking because he was getting all her business.

"I will, Honey," Ma said, waving.

With resentment, Emily watched her through the store window. Ma stopped to talk to Mrs. Thomas midway across the street. Mindless of the winter chill, Emily snatched up her broom and stomped to the front step, glaring at Jeremiah's false storefront.

My own ma, racing over to help the competition run me out of business. Honestly, the lack of loyalty was shameful. Of course, the thought of Christmas without Ma's sugar cookies or apple tarts was every bit the tragedy as sending a little business to Jeremy.

ﻬ

With a silent groan, Jeremiah watched Cassidy St. John heading across the street to his store. Sugar. He knew the only reason any of Emily's loyal family would be coming to Jeremiah's would be a shortage of one unavoidable item or another. In this case, it must be the sugar he had quite selflessly warned Emily to stock up on. But she had, as usual, failed to take his advice; and as a result, he'd practically had a run on the stuff.

Even now, he could see Em standing outside pretending to sweep, but anger was evidenced in the beating her broom took against the wooden step. He smiled to himself as a plan entered his mind; and from sheer glee, he extended his wide grin to one of his own loyal customers—compliments of Ma's League of Christian Women and their boycott of the "mannish" Emily St. John.

The last thought brought a chuckle to his lips. Emily—mannish.

"Let me take that crate out to the wagon for you, Mrs. Moody."

The elderly woman beamed up at him from rosy cheeks

and lovely, though faded blue eyes. *She must have been a real beauty in her day,* Jeremiah thought as she slipped a bony, veined hand through the crook of his arm and they walked slowly out the door.

What would Emily look like when she was old? Every bit as lovely, to be sure. He'd love the chance to find out, except that for some reason, ever since the harvest dance, Emily refused to so much as give him the time of day. He'd tried numerous times to have a chat with her, but she consistently evaded his efforts.

Once, he'd drummed up the courage to request the honor of escorting her to Sunday service and she'd politely refused, stating she saw no reason to dirty up the Lord's Day with pretense and deceit.

Still puzzled, Jeremiah shook his head at the memory. He'd been trying to figure it out ever since, but still found himself no closer to understanding her meaning than when she'd said it two weeks ago.

"Looks like you're doing quite well for yourself, Mr. Daniels," Mrs. Moody was saying. "We're all so pleased and proud at how you turned out, in spite of your early raisin'."

She patted his arm and let go as Mr. Moody climbed down and held out his hand to help her into the wagon.

Jeremiah stiffened at the reference to his childhood. Would there ever be those in town who couldn't remember his pa? Pa didn't even have drunkenness as an excuse. He had just been mean. That was the hardest reality for Jeremiah to wrap his mind around.

"Good morning, Mr. and Mrs. Moody!" Cassidy's cheery voice hailed the elderly couple as she stepped up to the wooden sidewalk in front of the store. Jeremiah welcomed her with a smile, relieved at the interruption. He didn't want to go down another winding road of dark and oppressive memory. Not now. Not ever. But sometimes the thoughts came; and when they did, he was hard-pressed to remember

St. Paul's instructions to bring "into captivity every thought to the obedience of Christ."

"Cassidy St. John. I never expected to see you on this side of the street," Mrs. Moody said with a chuckle.

"I'm afraid my daughter has sold out of sugar; and with the children coming next week for Christmas, I have quite a bit of baking to do." She smiled at Jeremiah. "She sent me to her old pal, with her blessing."

Jeremiah kept his expression as passive as he could, knowing just how hard it had been for Emily to send anyone, let alone her own mother, to his mercantile.

"That's my pal. Not a competitive bone in her body." He offered Cassidy his arm. "Shall we go inside and get you that sugar, Mrs. St. John?"

"Certainly. Good day," she said to the elderly couple before slipping her hand inside the crook of his arm.

Cassidy released him as soon as they entered the store. She looked nervously about, as though she felt like a traitor.

Jeremiah's heart went out to her, and he decided now was as good a time as any to implement his plans. "Mrs. St. John, can you wait until later for the sugar?"

She snapped to attention, her eyes widening. "You're not out too?"

"No. I have plenty. And I plan to sell Emily half of my stock. So you see, there's no need for you to buy it from me."

The delight on Cassidy's face brought heat to Jeremiah's neck. She touched his arm. "That's quite chivalrous of you. I know Emily will appreciate it a great deal."

Even if Jeremiah were a betting man, he wouldn't take that wager. Emily would be madder than a bull caught in a fence and would most likely refuse his offer, but he smiled and nodded. "Yes, Ma'am. Tell Em I'll be over later with half my stock."

"Maybe you better just tell her yourself." Cassidy gave him a rueful grin. "And while you're at it, ask her to put back ten pounds for me. I'll send Will in for it tomorrow."

Jeremiah waited until five o'clock and loaded a wheelbarrow with bags of sugar, then gathered a deep breath and headed over to Emily's Place.

a

Emily heard the bell above the door ding. Another customer she would have to send over to Jeremiah. She sighed and headed to the front of the store, stopping short at the sight that greeted her.

"What on earth?" Emily gasped. "Jeremiah! You—you're getting snow all over my floor! I demand you get that wheelbarrow outside this minute!"

Jeremiah let go of the wheelbarrow and straightened his back. He glanced around, then gave her a sheepish smile. "Sorry about the mud."

"What do you think you're doing?"

"Bringing you half my stock of sugar."

"I refuse to accept it!" She wouldn't accept charity from any man. Mrs. Thomas would never let her hear the end of it.

He grinned. "I'm not giving it to you. I'm selling it. At a profit to myself, of course." He named his price.

"Why, that's highway robbery!" Emily planted her hands indignantly on her hips. "I won't make a penny on it."

"At least you won't lose any more business. You know your customers are coming to me for sugar, but that's not all they're buying. I've cleaned up this week, thanks to your red-headed stubbornness."

Emily's temper flared, but she checked it. Even selling the sugar to her at a raised price, Jeremy wouldn't make as much as if he'd kept it for himself. The least she could do was swallow her pride and have the grace to thank him.

"I appreciate your generosity, Jeremiah."

He raised his brow in surprise, then his expression relaxed into a gentle smile. "It's my pleasure."

Emily cleared her throat and straightened her spine. "But

remember, I didn't ask for your help." She willed her pulse to slow to normal. She had to remember that Jeremiah's kindness had nothing to do with his feelings for her. He was only trying to woo her in order to get his hands on the mercantile.

He chuckled. "Don't worry. If anyone asks, I'll make sure they know you had to pay a hefty price for the sugar."

Although she tried her best to resist, laughter bubbled to her lips at the teasing glint in his eyes. Jeremiah understood perfectly well. He was more than a hero. He was a silent hero. She watched out the window as he pushed the wheelbarrow back to his store. In moments, he reappeared at his door and headed back in her direction. He waited for an oncoming wagon to pass before he crossed the street. Emily smiled. Yes, he was quite the hero.

She walked across the room and opened the door for him. The snowy air added just the right atmosphere for the Christmas season. She stepped into the frigid December air and frowned. Amelia Bell stood next to Jeremiah, obviously fishing for a tidbit of juicy news to print in her pa's newspaper. Emily wasn't sure how she felt about her so-called friend gaining recognition as Harper's first woman reporter. After all, her claim to fame so far had come at Emily's expense. Staring at the pixie-faced, bespectacled young woman, Emily remembered every article.

Price War! Head to Emily's Place for the best price on flour this week; but be careful, if you're looking for grain seed, take a short walk across the street and Jeremiah's will set you up right nicely.

Or the time Emily had ordered the orange-striped bonnets and material to match. Emily's cheeks burned at the memory.

Anyone looking for a costume for Mrs. Taylor's masquerade ball next month, consider the new bonnets at Emily's place. You're sure to win the prize for most atrocious getup.

And Emily didn't even want to think about the time she had decided Harper needed a little refinement. She'd decided to order fresh seafood. Twenty pounds of dead lobsters arrived much overdue after the train carrying them derailed and overturned.

Don't panic, good citizens of Harper. Large, red bugs aren't taking over our town. Hoping to tempt our taste buds, Emily's Place planned to offer lobster as an alternative to our common cuisine. Unfortunately, she didn't take into consideration the possibility of the train derailing.

Emily's humiliation had been complete when three schoolboys had swiped one of the odious shellfish and placed it on their new teacher's chair when she wasn't looking. In an uproar and quite in plain view, Miss Larkins had stomped over, deceased lobster in hand, and flung it on the counter, insisting Emily remove the temptation from her young students before the rest of the unfortunate lobsters ended up cleverly placed in various regions of the school.

Emily had waited until nightfall and grabbed her shovel. Jeremiah arrived and silently took the shovel from her. Without a word, he buried every one of those smelly things—deep enough so the dogs couldn't dig them up. Emily smiled at the memory. When he finished, he handed her the shovel, tweaked her nose, and left, never once scolding her for her unrealistic idea. Times such as those nearly convinced Emily that Jeremiah cared for her. But the memory of his conversation with Harold always brought her back to reality.

Emily watched him now, sidestepping Amelia's questions as to why the proprietor of one store would be bringing a shipment to his competition.

Jeremiah nudged his way around Emily and stepped into the mercantile. He sent her a silent plea for help. Emily grinned, tempted to let him handle the nosy reporter on his own, but her conscience got the better of her. Under the circumstances, the least she could do was head Amelia off.

"Morning, Amelia. Out for another fine story, today?"

"Oh, Emily. Jeremiah won't say a word. Tell me why on earth he is bringing you bags of sugar." She raised her voice slightly and cast a glance at Jeremiah as he stepped back through the door. "If you don't tell me, I'll be forced to assume."

"Assume what?" Emily asked.

"Oh, I don't know." Amelia tapped her lip with her forefinger, her eyes twinkling merrily. "Let me see. . . . Emily's Place has run out of a most important commodity during the holiday season and rather than profit at her expense, Jeremiah Daniels has put aside any hint of rivalry in the spirit of the season. . .or has he done so for another reason?"

A gasp escaped Emily's lips. "Don't you dare make implications about Jeremiah in that newspaper. He is helping me out because he's a decent man."

"And because I don't want to be called Scrooge a week before Christmas." Jeremiah flashed a heart-stopping grin as he unloaded the wheelbarrow.

Amelia gave Emily a knowing glance. "And of course because everyone knows you two are sweet on each other. There must be a headline in that. Sweet. . .sugar. How about, 'Sugar Isn't the Only Thing Sweet Going on Between Emily's Place and Jeremiah's'?"

Emily gasped. "Why, Amelia Bell! If you print that, I'll flat out deny it even if I have to place an ad in your pa's paper myself. And. . .and I'll never, ever place another advertisement in the Herald."

"Oh, Emily. Don't be silly. I'm teasing. I report real news. What do I care who you're courting?"

Stamping her foot in frustration, Emily glared. "We are not courting." She grabbed Jeremiah's arm as he stepped toward them, obviously intent on ducking out and leaving Emily to deal with Amelia. "Will you please tell her exactly why you are selling me half your sugar stock, Jeremy?"

Looking like an animal caught in a trap, Jeremiah swallowed hard. "Just the spirit of Christmas, I suppose."

"And he's charging me a hefty sum," Emily huffed, rather put out with Jeremiah for forcing her to be the one to mention the price while he stood looking like St. Nicholas bearing gifts. She gave him the fiercest of frowns and then turned back to the reporter. "Make sure you print that."

Jeremiah headed through the door. "Amelia."

"Yes?"

"You were right."

"What about?"

He grinned at Emily. "I am sweet on her. And you can print that as well." Before Emily could recover, he wheeled down the board he'd thrown over the steps, laid the board across the wheelbarrow, and went back to his store.

Amelia tossed back her head and let out a hearty laugh. "There you have it, Emily. I told you he was smitten. What do you have to say about that?" She followed Emily back inside. "I'll bet he proposes by New Year."

"It doesn't matter when he proposes. My answer will be no."

"Are you crazy?" Amelia grabbed a bag of sugar and slid it on the counter. "Why on earth are you playing coy with Jeremiah? Are you honestly considering playing hard to get, at your age?"

Emily sent her a scowl. "You don't know all the facts, Amelia. Trust me when I say, I am not playing games. I have my reasons for keeping Jeremiah at bay; and I have no intention of sharing those intentions with a newspaper reporter, so you may as well get that inquisitive look off your face."

The hopeful expression on Amelia's face dropped like a disappointed child's.

Emily sent her an indulgent smile. "How about telling me about you and Clyde? He's been escorting you to church quite a bit since the dance. Rumor has it, you're courting quite regularly."

A pretty blush crossed Amelia's cheeks. "I suppose ol' Clyde's not so bad after all. And he says I can work for Pa two days a week even after we're married as long as the boys are in school."

"Oh, Amelia, how wonderful. I'm so thrilled for you!"

And she was truly happy for her friend, but her heart ached just a little with the knowledge that there seemed to be love for everyone but her. It appeared the best she could hope for was a man who wanted her mainly for her business. But listening to Amelia's happy plans, for the first time Emily was beginning to wonder if perhaps it would be worth giving up the store to become Jeremiah's wife.

But could she honestly live with the knowledge that she was nothing more than a means to an end for him?

Her frustrated huff earned her a surprised glance from Amelia.

Emily gave her an apologetic smile. No, she wanted true love. And while she'd happily share the store with a man who loved her, she refused to simply give it away to a gold digger.

seven

The day after Christmas, Jeremiah stood in the middle of his store, nostrils flared. Anger tore through him like an eagle's talons as he glanced around the disorderly store. He'd been the victim of a break-in. Who on earth had done such a thing?

He gathered a breath and straightened an overturned barrel. Thankfully, it had only been filled with an assortment of garden tools rather than pickles or something equally messy.

As he set the room in order, Jeremiah mentally took stock of the items on the shelves and tables. He sent up a prayer of thanks that he routinely emptied the cash box each night, so there had been no money for a thief to take. Casting another quick glance from one end of the room to the other, he reached back and kneaded his neck.

Not a thing had been stolen.

As a matter of fact. . .

Perplexed, he strode the length of the room for a closer look at the bags of sugar piled in front of the counter. He scratched his head, trying to grasp the fact that there were twice as many as when he had left work the night before last, on Christmas Eve.

Had Emily brought back her unsold bags? Immediately he rejected the ludicrous thought. Why would she break in to do that? And besides, she had sent her little sister, Hope, over with payment in full the day after he'd made his delivery.

Though it made no sense, he had to conclude someone had broken into both stores—had stolen from Emily and given to him.

He glanced through the window to Emily's Place. Had she found a similar mess when she arrived this morning? Knowing how easily she became frightened, Jeremiah set his lips into a grim line and debated whether he should go over there or not. The thought of her afraid made his heart clench and settled the matter. After making sure the door was securely locked, Jeremiah strode across the street and climbed the steps to the familiar store. He reached for the doorknob, then hesitated as he remembered the look of horror on Emily's face when he'd admitted his feelings. What had possessed him to reveal such a thing, he'd never know. . .not in a million years. But he certainly didn't relish the idea of Emily railing at him about it. It was probably a blessing that she'd have something else upon which to focus her attention.

Taking a deep breath, he opened the door. Emily stood in the center of the store, sweeping up what looked to be sugar from the wood floor.

She glared. "Really, Jeremiah. If you didn't want to sell me the sugar, all you had to do was ask for it back."

Jeremiah gaped. "You think I did this?"

A shrug lifted her shoulders. "Who else? I assume you sold out and didn't want to lose money until the supply train arrives at the end of the week. Now, if you'll excuse me, I've lost an hour's business because of this mess. And it appears I have a customer."

Emily leaned the broom against the wall. When she turned around, her face showed about as much warmth as the ice hanging from the barn awnings this morning. "I'll thank you to return your key." To her credit, she lowered her voice as the bell dinged above the door.

Jeremiah scowled at his inability to defend himself, as Amelia Bell stepped through the door.

"Good morning, Jeremiah," she said, a smirk tipping the corners of her lips. "Aren't you on the wrong side of the street?"

"Yes, I think so," he said, striding purposefully toward the door.

Emily was the most stubborn, pigheaded woman he'd ever

known. How in the world could she imagine he'd steal back his own sugar? With a scowl, Jeremiah snatched open the door. For now, he'd get his own store ready for customers, and he'd come back later to return her sugar—and the key he'd held to Tucker's Mercantile since he was a kid.

"Good day, ladies."

Emily's "harrumph" followed him out the door and down the steps. It stayed in his mind all the way across the street, fueling his indignation into an angry fire. By the time he unlocked his door and grabbed his apron, Jeremiah was downright mad. Who did Miss Emily St. John think she was, accusing him of stealing from her? It was so ridiculous that it might have been funny except that he never would have dreamed she could think so little of him.

His mind returned to the last time Emily had confronted him for stealing. . .only that time it had been warranted.

They had been ten years old, and even then she was the only girl he cared anything about. During a short devotional at school, Jeremiah had been pricked by the Holy Spirit and had admitted to stealing sourballs from Tucker's.

Emily's shock had pierced Jeremiah's heart like an arrow, but he'd known from that time on he'd never steal again. . . . And he had given his heart to Jesus that day.

Did she think his faith was nothing more than a cover? She must believe him to be a fake, a hypocrite.

The thought cut him deeply.

Throughout the rest of the day, Jeremiah had difficulty concentrating on his customers, as he pondered who was behind the silly robbery. More and more, he was coming to believe it must have been a schoolboy prank. Who else but an ornery boy would go to the trouble?

The more he thought about it, the more the whole situation struck a familiar chord. He grinned. From the standpoint of a child, it was sort of funny—a stroke of prank genius, stealing from one store and putting the goods in the other store.

Maybe he could get Emily to see it from that perspective. He doubted it. But maybe. . .

❧

Emily's face warmed, and she tried, without success, to remove the memory of her awful words to Jeremiah. How on earth could she accuse him of stealing anything, let alone something he'd been kind enough to share in the first place? Of course he had charged her a vulgar sum for the sugar when the truly charitable thing to do would have been to give it to her at cost; but then, he was a businessman and a good one at that. A rueful grin tipped the corners of her lips, though there was no one around to witness. Under the same circumstances, she most likely would have charged him the same.

And if she were honest with herself, she'd have to admit that her anger toward him was rooted in the fact that she already resented him for his intentions toward her and the store. She was holding a huge grudge; and while she wasn't quite ready to lower her guard where his pretend affections were concerned, she could at least apologize for accusing him of stealing.

With a glance at the clock, Emily noted there were only three minutes until closing time. She wanted to see Jeremiah before he locked up and headed toward his farm. He deserved an apology.

Emily grabbed her key and walked toward the door. Snow had begun to fall early in the day. Already the ground was quilted in the white fluff.

On a whim, she rubbed a circle on the frosty window and ventured a glance across the street, which seemed eerily still except for the occasional wagon rattling along, forming double trails in the fresh snow. Daylight had faded, giving way to a smoky twilight, which promised another moonless night.

Emily shuddered and debated the idea of going out alone. Just as she made up her mind to stay inside where it was warm, Jeremiah appeared in his window. Emily gasped and stepped back, then chided herself for her own silliness. She lifted her arm and returned his wave.

Observing him now as he watched the snow falling to the street outside, Emily decided to make a trip to Jeremiah's after all. But she'd have to hurry if she was to return home before complete darkness settled over the quiet town. Propriety demanded she not remain alone with Jeremiah in a darkened room. Regardless of the Equal Suffrage Association's outcry that women should have the freedom to decide for themselves what constituted a compromising situation, Emily didn't want to put herself or Jeremiah in that position.

At the thought of impropriety, she was about to change her mind yet again when Jeremiah gave her another wave.

"All right, Lord. Of course I know Jeremiah deserves an apology. I'll take his showing up in the window as Your way of telling me not to put off what needs to be said."

Before she could grab her cape, the bell dinged. She turned to see Mr. Moody stomping snow from his boots against the rag rugs in front of the door. "Evening," he said. "That cold wind cuts right to the bone."

"What can I get for you?"

"The missus says her shoulder's aching something fierce. You know what that means. Means we're about to have a storm, and she's out of yarn for knitting. Says she can't be sitting for days without something to occupy her fingers."

Emily's lips twitched. Mrs. Moody and her aching shoulder had been predicting storms with about a ten-percent accuracy rating for as long as she could remember, but Mr. Moody never failed to believe her predictions.

She finished with the elderly man, then grabbed her cape from behind the counter. Steeling herself against what was sure to be a blast of cold, Emily stepped outside. She wrapped her arms about her waist as the wind bit into her. Mr. Moody had been right about the biting wind. In moments, the snow had gone from soft flakes to a swirling mass of white.

By the time Emily reached the middle of the street, she was

shivering violently. Alarm seized her as the wind picked up and whipped mercilessly at her skirts, twisting them about her legs. She stumbled, but caught her balance just in time to avoid plunging headlong into the snowy street.

She braved a glance up, the snow stinging her eyes and cheeks like pellets. The soft glow from Jeremiah's window provided a beacon for her against the blinding white.

Only a few more steps and Jeremiah will be there. The thought urged her legs to move forward. The door opened just as she stepped up onto the icy boardwalk.

"Emily!" Jeremiah's voice sent waves of relief through her. "What were you thinking, heading out in this storm?" he admonished.

"I—I'm f–f–fine," she replied, grateful to be ushered inside the warm store, which smelled of saddle oil and sawdust. "I h–have to tell you something."

He led her to a chair next to a beautiful, coal-burning stove. "Here, sit down and warm up, then you can tell me what you risked frostbite to say. I'll be back." He walked to the window, looked out, then returned to where Emily sat. He smiled, but not before Emily observed his clouded expression and knew the snow worried him.

Jeremiah grabbed a mug from the shelf behind the counter and filled it with steaming coffee, which simmered on the stove. Emily gratefully accepted the mug, relishing the warmth against her half-frozen fingers.

"Thank you."

Jeremiah perched on a pickle barrel near the stove. He folded his arms across his chest and stretched his long legs out in front of him. He regarded her, his expression soft and welcoming—not at all what Emily would have expected from a man wrongly accused as he faced his accuser.

Emily found herself at a loss for words as she stared into his brown eyes.

"What brings you here on a night like this?" he prompted.

Dropping her gaze to the mug, Emily fought against sudden tears of remorse. "I just. . ." She gathered a steadying breath and raised her chin, meeting his gaze. "I wanted to apologize for my rudeness this morning."

A tender smile curved his full lips, and Emily's stomach turned a somersault.

"It's big of you to come by. But it wasn't necessary."

"It was. You're not a thief, and I had no right to make the accusation." She shook her head. "Sometimes, I just don't know why I say the things I do, Jeremiah." Emily's gaze sought his. "You've known me since we were children. Why do I always have to be the one who spouts in anger, only to regret it in the next moment?"

"I don't know, Em. But if it's bothering you, maybe you should learn to think before you speak. God will help you if you're honest about wanting to change."

Emily stiffened under the criticism, but relaxed as she studied his expression and found no malice. Releasing a heavy sigh, she nodded. "You're right."

His brow shot up and his mouth widened into a grin. "Too bad Amelia's not here to hear you. That has to be newsworthy."

In spite of herself, Emily giggled. "It's probably not as interesting as the crate of dead lobsters."

Jeremiah's pleasant laugh rang throughout the store, filling Emily with contentment. She added her laughter to his, and not until tears clouded her eyes did she gain control of her mirth.

"I don't remember the last time I laughed so hard. My sides absolutely ache." She smiled up at him, relishing the pleasantness of his returning smile.

He cleared his throat and stood. "Well, I better get you back across the street before it gets any darker. We don't want tongues wagging, do we?"

Emily's heart plummeted. Though she knew he was right, she couldn't help but feel a little let down. If only it were possible, she could have spent hours sitting in front of the stove and laughing with Jeremiah.

With a nod, she stood and handed him the mug. "Thank you for the coffee."

He set the cup on the counter, grinned, and looked about to speak when a blast of wind shook the store and the door blew open. Emily gasped as the snow swirled inside. Jeremiah hastened across the room and forced the door shut against the strong wind.

"I better hurry before that storm gets any worse," Emily said, dreading the thought of going out into the fierce snow.

"Emily," Jeremiah said hesitantly, "you can't go out in this."

"What do you mean? I have to go out, or I can't get home."

"Listen to that wind. I barely got the door closed. You wouldn't stand up for a second out there. I'm sorry, but there's no choice. You'll have to stay here until the storm is over." He motioned her back to the stove.

"It's dark out there! I can't stay any longer." Emily jerked away and headed back to the door.

Jeremiah caught her by her arms and demanded her gaze, his eyes showing fear. "I couldn't see past the walk outside. If you try to go outside, you'll be lost before you've gone five feet. How many times have you heard of friends and neighbors getting lost in a blizzard, only to be found a few feet from their house when the storm is over?"

Emily wilted against him as though all her fight was gone at the truth of his words.

"But how can you even suggest I stay here, considering your mother is the president of the League of Christian Women? What on earth would she and the rest of the league have to say about me? The things they already say are bad enough." She despised the break in her voice, but pretending the harsh judgments didn't hurt was impossible. Especially when facing the probability of even harsher judgments should she remain alone with a man—let alone Mrs. Daniels's son—for even minutes past dark.

Jeremiah regarded her with a tender smile, then he grabbed his coat, gloves, a hat, and a scarf.

"What are you doing?" Emily asked.

"You're right. We can't stay here together. It isn't possible to get you across the street safely, so I'm going to feel along the wall outside. The jail's only two doors down. I can make it there and pass the time with the sheriff. If you have to stay here until morning, use whatever you need from the shelves to stay comfortable. There's extra coal in back for the stove."

Knowing there was no other choice, Emily walked him to the door. "B—be careful, Jeremy."

He winked, sending her heart soaring. "I'll be fine."

Minutes later, he returned, his eyelashes frosted with ice, his cheeks red. His teeth chattered, and he shivered violently as he made his way to the stove and stood as close as he could, trying to get warm. When he could talk, he gave her a soulful smile. "I'm sorry, Emily. Jail's closed up and locked. I couldn't get in. We're going to have to stay here together."

"B—but what about your ma?"

"Let me handle my ma. I'll do everything I can to ensure your reputation is intact when the storm blows over. Maybe the snow will stop soon, and we can get you home before anyone even knows."

The thought was of little comfort, considering how the wind howled outside. "Please, Jeremiah." Emily made no effort to hide the tears welling in her eyes. "You can't imagine what it's like to be an outcast."

He started to reach for her, then apparently thought better of it and dropped his arm to his side. "Honey, I'm sorry, but you've lived in these parts long enough to know a blizzard when you see one. We'll have to wait it out and hope folks understand. And who knows? It could let up soon and I'll walk you home."

Emily heard his words, but she refused to entertain the thought that it was now past twilight and she and Jeremiah were alone.

eight

To Jeremiah, almost as worrisome as the raging storm outside was the sight of Emily huddled against the far wall. Worse still was the knowledge that she did so for fear he might get too close. She'd sat there for the last three hours, shivering and hugging her body tightly in an effort to foster warmth from her own arms.

"This is ridiculous, Em. Come over by the stove and warm up. You know I'm not going to touch you."

She sat up straighter and spoke through chattering teeth. "If anyone comes to find me, it'll look better if I'm all the way across the room from you." She sent him a knowing look. "Less opportunity for folks to talk."

Jeremiah surveyed the frost-covered wall behind her, wishing for all he was worth that he'd taken better care to insulate the store rather than trying to cut costs. "You'll freeze to death before anyone has a chance to talk if you stay over there."

She jerked her chin up and leveled her green-eyed gaze at him. "At least I'll die with my reputation intact."

"Have it your way." With a chuckle, he grabbed a couple of coats from the table and strode across the room. Allowing for no objections, he placed them over her until she was covered from chin to toes. "But if it's all the same to you, I'd just as soon you live to enjoy the favor of the good townspeople."

"Thank you, Jeremiah." Emily's smile almost undid his resolve to keep his distance. Quickly, he moved back to the window and glanced out at the angry storm.

The wind howled with vicious fervor and shook the store, rattling the front window until Jeremiah feared it might not hold up.

"I'm going to have to board up that glass," he said, more to himself than to Emily.

"I think you'd better. I certainly hope my glass holds up. I dread the thought of what I might find when the storm quits." Emily stood and carefully laid the coats in a pile. "In any case, I'll help you get yours covered. That'll give us something to do for awhile."

"Thanks," Jeremiah replied, wishing he could gather her into his arms and melt away the look of worry from her eyes. "I could use it."

He strode to the storeroom and retrieved four large slats.

"Where did those come from?"

"Lionel McDonald ordered these. He intends to build a small house this spring."

"He ordered a shipment of wood from you?" Emily's eyes flashed in sudden outrage. "Why, I'd have sold it to him at a better price. I don't see why he's wasting money anyway. Most young couples start off in soddies or sandstone homes."

"The soon-to-be Mrs. McDonald flatly refuses to live in a soddy. And I highly doubt the young groom wants to take time to haul enough sandstone from the creek for a house. He'll gladly part with the money to make her happy."

"Why do you suppose his new bride isn't coming until summer?" Emily asked.

Distracted by her wrinkled nose and brow crinkled in thought, Jeremiah failed to stop and weigh his words. "She's waiting until her sister gives birth and gains her strength, from what I understand."

Emily pinkened, and Jeremiah suppressed a smile. She might be a forward-thinking woman, but even Emily-the-suffragette couldn't escape the modesty of a gentle upbringing. She cleared her throat. "Oh, well, I suppose that's understandable."

Jeremiah handed her the bag of nails and a hammer. "Hold these until I ask for them, okay?"

With a nod, she accepted the items; and they worked

together in silence until the window was covered. Jeremiah only prayed that the wind didn't shatter the glass on the other side of the boards. Replacing it would be an expense he certainly didn't need.

"That ought to do it." He stepped back to survey their handiwork. He took the nail bag and hammer from Emily and put them away in the storeroom. When he returned, Emily was standing next to the stove, her hands stretched toward the little warmth offered.

"It's getting colder in here," he mused. "I'm sorry. But I think it's best to conserve coal as much as possible. How about covering up?"

Emily nodded. She grabbed two coats from the pile by the wall and handed him one. "You too."

His heart lurched, and he knew he could no more have refused to accept the gesture than the wind could fail to blow if God so ordained. His gaze captured hers; and to his amazement, she didn't look away. On the contrary, she seemed as mesmerized as he. Jeremiah drew in a sharp breath, and a shiver slid up his spine as he made a startling discovery. Did Emily care for him? Was it even possible that she felt the way he did?

Her eyes welcomed him to become lost in their green depths, and he knew he was treading dangerous waters. Better to be in the blizzard than faced with the temptation that presented itself to him at this moment—the woman of his heart who could very likely be forced to share the same building for the night, if the storm didn't let up soon.

Suddenly Jeremiah was faced with a weakness he had no idea afflicted him.

If Emily had remained haughty or angry or even fragile, he might never have considered the fullness of her lips or the roundness of her figure. He might never have imagined pulling her to him and kissing her, holding her. But his mind grabbed onto the image and he couldn't let it go. Wordlessly, he stared. He took a step toward her, fully aware he should be moving in the other direction.

"Jeremiah?" Even in a shaky whisper, his name had never sounded so sweet coming from any other lips. "Please don't come any closer."

He closed his eyes to gain control.

Help us, Lord. Deliver us from evil and temptation. We both belong to You, and neither of us would choose to be in a situation where we might sin against You.

In an instant, his stomach grumbled loudly.

He opened his eyes. Emily giggled. And the moment passed.

"I reckon I'm hungry," he announced with a grin. "Let's see what I can find for us." Still fighting to gain control over his raw emotions, Jeremiah surveyed the shelves critically, thankful for the excuse to focus on anything but Emily. "We can open a can of beans."

Emily wrinkled her nose. "There's always candy," Jeremiah said, unable to suppress his grin.

"Licorice sticks for supper. Every child's dream." Emily good-naturedly helped herself from a jar on the counter.

"There's always a chance the storm will let up; but in case it doesn't, we should face the possibility of being here for a couple of days." Jeremiah frowned and released a breath. "There are plenty of canned goods, so food won't be a problem."

"I can even pull together the ingredients for bread or biscuits." Emily cast a quick glance at the shelves. "From the looks of your stock, we could live on that until the spring thaw. Of course, I'd expect you to charge me for my share."

A chuckle rose up in Jeremiah at the teasing glint in her eyes. "Don't think I won't."

She smiled back, and they fell silent once again. Unwilling to be put in the position to allow temptation to get another grip on them, Jeremiah broke eye contact almost immediately. "I best go and bring in some coal from the back. I'll build the fire up a bit to keep us warm until the storm passes." Which, from the sounds of the wind, wouldn't be anytime soon. Jeremiah scooped coal into the stove, and soon warmth radiated through the back part of the store.

"Jeremiah?"

Turning at the sound of Emily's voice, Jeremiah's heart picked up. The worry in her eyes filled him with compassion. "What is it, Honey?"

"Is your ma going to be okay?"

He'd been worrying about the same thing. But Ma was resourceful. There was plenty of food to keep her, plenty of coal for at least two weeks.

"She has everything she needs." He gave her a wry grin. " 'Course with no one to talk to until this is over, I might be in for a lengthy conversation when I see her."

Emily giggled, then they fell silent again. Jeremiah gave a satisfied sigh that even with Emily's opposing viewpoints, she had thought of his mother being alone at the farm. He smiled into the silence.

After hours of listening to the howling wind, Emily sat in the chair, silently staring at the wall until Jeremiah noticed her eyelids drooping. A wide yawn stretched her mouth. "You might as well go to sleep, Em. This storm isn't quitting, and there's no sense in staying awake all night. It's already after midnight. Let's make a place for you to sleep."

Emily shot from the chair, eyeing him warily. "I have a place to sleep." She glanced toward the wall and the three coats still piled on the floor.

"It's too cold over there."

"Well, I'm not sleeping close to you, Jeremiah."

After the silent exchange between them earlier, he couldn't really blame her for not trusting him to keep a respectable distance. Still, she'd catch her death sleeping next to the wall in the coldest part of the store. Bad enough that her reputation would be in question after a night alone with him.

Jeremiah released a heavy sigh. There was nothing to be done about the situation. "I promise not to come near you."

She squared her shoulders and headed for the wall as though he hadn't spoken. "I've made up my mind, and there's no point in trying to change it. This is for the best."

She made a pallet of coats and started to lower herself. She hesitated. "Do you want some of these?"

"No, I have this one plus I'm sleeping next to the stove. I'll be plenty warm."

"Have it your way, then." She stretched out and covered up, turning her back to him. "Please don't watch me. It makes me nervous."

Heat crept up Jeremiah's neck. He averted his gaze and settled onto the floor, resting his back against a barrel. From time to time, he found himself watching Emily. She struggled to find a comfortable position; and even under two coats, she shivered.

Finally after two hours of intermittently watching her fight against cold, Jeremiah stood and grabbed the remaining blankets from a stack on the shelf. When he had made a pallet several inches thick, Jeremiah walked toward Emily.

☙

Emily felt herself being lifted into warm arms. She sighed, relishing the dream. Suddenly reality broke through, and she opened her eyes. Jeremiah stared at her, his face merely inches from hers.

She gasped as she realized this was no dream. "What do you think you're doing?"

"Getting you away from that cold wall whether you like it or not." He spoke without even a hint of an apology.

"Put me down this instant."

"I intend to," he said, his voice clipped as he lowered her to her feet. "Now, lie down and go back to sleep."

Emily's eyes grew wide. "What is this?"

"A warm place to sleep. I suggest you put it to good use."

Setting the poker aside, he turned to her, his expression almost pleading. "Please just lay down. I will keep my distance, I promise."

Unable to withstand his earnest appeal, Emily nodded. She lowered herself to the pallet, guiltily settling into the soft warmth. By all rights, Jeremiah should be enjoying this. But she knew it would be pointless to suggest he take it, and of course sharing it was out of the question. Her cheeks burned at the fleeting thought, and suddenly her mind reverted to the moment between them when she'd thought for sure he would kiss her. Relief and disappointment had mingled when his stomach grumbled, breaking off the intensity of the silence that had spoken more than words could have. Oh, if only she could believe he truly cared for her.

Heavy, even breathing reached her; and Emily looked up to see Jeremiah seated on the floor, his back and head resting against a barrel. He still wore his coat, but Emily knew he'd be cold when he woke up after the fire had died down. She peeled off two blankets from her pallet. Walking the few feet across to Jeremiah, she carefully covered him.

She tiptoed back to her pallet and laid down.

"Thank you." Jeremiah's husky, sleepy voice reached her ears like a warm breeze. Knowing she dare not face him, Emily forced herself to remain with her back to him. She drifted to sleep with a smile on her lips.

For the next three days, the wind howled and snow whirled about outside. Utilizing Jeremiah's stock, Emily baked biscuits and even made gravy. Although there was no meat to go with their meals, Jeremiah vowed he had never eaten so well. Emily blushed at his compliments. Gradually they became comfortable in each other's presence, settling into a familiar pattern.

At night they slept much like the first night. During the day, Emily insisted Jeremiah nap on her pallet.

Finally, on the fourth day, the howling wind quieted; and

after a few hours, Jeremiah decided to remove the boards from the window. Emily held her breath as the first board came loose. White nothingness stared back at them.

"Oh, my." She put her hand to her mouth.

"The drifts must be as high as the window," Jeremiah said grimly. "I can't see anything but snow."

"Do you want to try the door?" Emily heard the shake in her voice.

After several attempts, Jeremiah shook his head and glanced at her helplessly. He tried the back door and met the same lack of success. "I'm sorry. It won't budge. It must be iced over on the outside. But now that the snow has stopped, others will be able to get out, I'm sure. You know your pa will hook up the sleigh and get into town as soon as he can to make sure you're fine. Someone will dig us out soon. If not today, then tomorrow or the next day for sure."

Emily inwardly groaned at the thought of being cooped up for two or three more days. Not that the last few days with Jeremiah hadn't been pleasant enough despite the forced circumstances. But she was ready to breathe fresh air again.

Her shoulders lifted in a resigned shrug. "Well, then I suppose I should mix up another batch of biscuits."

Jeremiah stopped her with a soft grip on her upper arm. "I'd like to talk to you about something. I suppose now is as good a time as any."

Emily returned his gaze, wondering at the seriousness in his brown eyes. "Yes?"

"After this many days alone, there will be no stopping tongues from wagging. You realize that, right?"

Heat rose to her cheeks. "Yes." Tears burned in her eyes. Why did he have to bring up the reminder of her coming humiliation?

He cleared his throat and took both of her hands in his. "I want you to know that I understand my responsibility to you."

"Responsibility?"

Nodding, he squeezed her hands. "As soon as we can get out, we'll head straight to the parsonage. Anthony can perform the ceremony right away."

Confusion clouded Emily's mind. She blinked up at him. "What ceremony?"

A frown creased Jeremiah's brow. "Our marriage ceremony, of course."

nine

"Marriage? Jeremiah Daniels, that's the most utterly ridiculous thing I've ever heard you say!" He understood his responsibility? Emily fumed. He understood a good way to get his hands on her business. That was what he understood! "I have no intention of marrying you now or ever."

Jeremiah's brow rose, and he released her from his grip. "What do you mean? You know as well as I do, we have no choice. Think of the scandal this will cause. What of your pa's position in town?"

Emily gave a sniff. "You mean your ma's position."

"Yes, partly." Jeremiah's steady gaze burned into Emily with a stubbornness she had rarely seen. He meant business. "My ma was the town talk before my pa died because everyone knew how he treated us. And after he died, they talked about her because of my actions before Tuck hired me at the mercantile. The last thirteen years, she's slowly risen to a place of respectability. I won't allow her to lose her standing among those self-righteous hens if belonging there makes her so happy."

"Need I remind you of my standing in the community?" Emily huffed, wishing desperately this proposal of marriage were being made for any other reason in the whole world—especially when her heart raced at the thought of becoming Jeremiah's bride. Still, she had to get out of it with her pride intact. She absolutely couldn't endure the humiliation of anyone knowing exactly why Jeremiah really wanted to marry her. "What would my association think if I let a man force me into marriage simply because we were trapped and innocently spent a few days together?"

"I don't see how that compares, Em. The League of Christian Women is made up of all the respectable women in town. You've been on thin ice with them for the last year, as it is. You'll completely lose your good name if you don't marry me."

"Are you threatening me, Jeremiah Daniels? Because if you are—"

"Threatening? You take my marriage proposal as a threat?"

"Proposal? Your so-called proposal was barbaric. Another example of a male-dominated society!" Emily flailed her arms, pacing the floor and feeling as though she might explode any second. She whirled around and faced him, then deepened her voice in a poor imitation. "You have to marry me. I'm not asking, I'm telling."

"I think you've gone soft in the head from being shut up in the store too long."

"You see? I'm the one who's gone soft in the head because I didn't throw myself into your arms and declare undying gratitude that you want to spare your mother's reputation."

Jeremiah opened his mouth to reply, but Emily continued without giving him the chance to speak.

"Never mind that I might not think it's the best idea. Never mind that we've never once spoken of love. Never mind that you've never asked me to a dance or asked my pa for permission to court me."

Emily's lip trembled. Oh those tears! Those dreadful, tell-tale tears.

Jeremiah stepped forward and gently took her hands in his. "Em, look at me."

Stubbornly, Emily kept her gaze on the tips of her boots.

A long sigh left Jeremiah's lips. "All right. Don't look at me, but at least listen to what I have to say."

"Say it, then."

"I would have courted you if I had thought you wanted me to."

Emily ventured a glance upward. His eyes held a look of earnest appeal. Her mind screamed for her to stay strong, not to give in to his obvious attempt to ensnare her with talk of courting and romance—especially when she knew the truth; but her rebellious heart couldn't help but venture on, exploring where the conversation might lead.

With tenderness, he studied her face, searching for truth as much as Emily searched for the same from him. "Would you have said yes?"

"I let you kiss me when we were sixteen," she mumbled. "What did you think that was, if not a hint that I'd accept you as a beau?"

He chuckled. "I heard you and Amelia Bell talking by the punch bowl that night. She dared you to kiss the first boy who tried."

A gasp escaped Emily's lips. He was right. "I'd completely forgotten about that." She'd forgotten everything about that night except for Jeremiah's soft, warm kiss. But now her mind conjured the memory of what had led up to the event. "My brother Luke had stolen a kiss from Amelia right under the kissing tree, and she was bragging about it. That was long before Laney lassoed him in, of course."

"If I recall correctly," Jeremiah said wryly, "Laney didn't have to lasso him too tightly to bring him in."

"That's true." Emily smiled. "Some people just belong together." Her heart ached to admit it.

"Yes, they do." Though his voice rang with emotion, Emily refused to try to discover whether his words held a double meaning. Better to take them at face value and conclude he meant Luke and Laney belonged together than to have her hopes dashed. Instead, she continued reliving the memory of the night of their one and only kiss. "Anyway, I told Amelia kissing wasn't anything to brag about, she should be ashamed for letting him do it in the first place, and I had half a mind to tell my ma on Luke." Emily giggled. "I think Amelia's dare was mainly to keep from getting into trouble with her own pa if word got out she'd been kissing anyone. She knew I wouldn't turn down a dare."

"Lucky for me I happened to be listening in on the conversation. I had to force myself to wait a respectable amount of time so you wouldn't know I'd been eavesdropping."

"Why, Jeremiah Daniels, you took advantage of me!"

His face split into a rakish grin. "What else would you expect a smitten young man to do? I'd be a disgrace to the male gender if I hadn't taken the opportunity when it presented itself."

"A smitten young man?" Emily sniffed. "If you were so smitten, why did it take a dare to induce you to ask me to dance?"

"That's pretty obvious, isn't it? Can you imagine Emily St. John, daughter of one of the town's most prominent citizens, courting me? I knew I wasn't good enough for you. And likely everyone else did too. I could have asked, but I seriously doubt your pa would have allowed me to court you."

Emily's heart pounded furiously. She narrowed her gaze. "Then you don't know the first thing about my family! My pa would no more hold your past against you than he would put one of his grandchildren on a bucking horse."

He released a long breath. "Then maybe I should have asked, but stigma is an almost impossible thing to overcome. Don't you see? That's why you have to marry me. Our families would have to defend us and themselves for a long, long time if we don't make this right."

Disappointment washed through Emily, draining her strength. She turned away and grabbed a bag of flour from the counter. "Forget it, Jeremiah. When I marry, I want a decent proposal from a man who's in love with me. My family would never expect me to marry just to keep tongues from wagging."

Emily heard the clip of quick, booted steps behind her, and her heart picked up. Before she had the opportunity to face him, she felt Jeremiah's hands on her shoulders turning her around.

He pulled her close, his face inches from hers. "You're too stubborn for your own good." His hands moved up her shoulders and cupped her neck, his thumbs caressing the lines of her jaw. "You have no idea how I feel about you. Perhaps it's my own fault for keeping quiet all these years."

Emily closed her eyes, blanketed in the soft warmth of his hands. For a moment, she pushed aside all thoughts of whether or not Jeremiah had ulterior motives, and she abandoned herself to the pleasure of his closeness. The tenderness.

"So help me, Emily. . ." In one agonizingly long second, their breath mingled, just before his lips claimed hers.

This was no repeat of a long-ago schoolboy's kiss. Soft, but filled with passion, Jeremiah's lips moved over hers until Emily's head swam. Childhood memories fled her mind, along with the reality of the snow outside and the last few days. They were alone in an uncomplicated world where there was no room for worrying about scandal or trying to gauge Jeremiah's reasons for asking her to marry him.

A sudden chill swept into the room, and Emily frowned as Jeremiah's lips left hers.

They turned toward the back door, the direction of the cold air. Emily gasped. Jeremiah pulled her close into the protective circle of his arms. In the doorway stood every male member of Emily's family, glaring and poised for action.

&

Jeremiah saw his mangled, bruised body reflected in the angry glares burning at him from the doorway. He cleared his throat and tightened his grip on Emily's shoulder.

"Sir," he said, addressing Dell, "I assure you this isn't what it looks like."

Dell stepped across the threshold and closed the distance between them in a few long strides. "That's a good thing for you, Son, because let me tell you what it looks like from my perspective."

Jeremiah swallowed hard, fully anticipating the situation from a pa's point of view.

"From where I stood—and correct me if I'm wrong—it looked like you had your arms around my daughter and were kissing her—and not just a chaste peck on the cheek. You were kissing her a little too deeply for my comfort."

"Oh, Pa, really. It wasn't anything."

Jeremiah leaned in and spoke close to her ear. "What do you mean it wasn't anything? It was something to me."

"Would you be quiet?" Emily glared up at him. "I'm trying to save you from getting a behind full of buckshot."

Loud guffaws coming from the doorway pulled Jeremiah's attention from Emily. He frowned.

"I don't see what's funny about this situation." He turned to Anthony, Emily's brother-in-law. "I'm glad you're here, Reverend Greene. It'll save us a trip to the parsonage in the cold."

"It's good to see you intend to do the honorable thing," Dell said, nodding his cool approval. "But I think Emily's ma and sisters will want to be in attendance when you actually say the vows."

Jeremiah scowled, knowing every day that passed would give the gossips more time to talk. "I suppose we could wait a day or two, as long as the townsfolk realize a wedding is going to take place directly and that any delay is your idea, not mine. I'm more than ready to do right by your daughter, Sir. And rest assured that the scene you walked in on was the only one of its kind that happened over the last few days."

"It's good to hear that." Dell turned his attention to Emily, who stood red-faced and teary-eyed. "Get your coat, Sweetheart. I have the sleigh outside ready to take us home to your ma. You've no idea how worried she's been."

He extended his hand to Jeremiah. "We'll be in touch about the wedding."

"Now, hold on just a minute!" Emily stomped one foot on the floor and planted her hands firmly on her hips. "I've never agreed to any kind of marriage. Jeremiah and I were trapped together—but not by choice. The blizzard just came on so suddenly, all we could do was wait it out. Nothing happened between us that would warrant suspicion and the need to marry." Her face grew a darker shade of red. "Well, all right, that kiss happened; but honestly, if the boys had to marry every girl they kissed under the kissing tree, they'd all have a dozen wives."

The boys laughed. "She has a point, there, Pa," seventeen-year-old Will said with a wide grin.

"What would you know about it, Little Bit?" Jack asked, elbowing his brother in the ribs.

"You trying to say I've never kissed a girl?" Will's face reddened, and he stood poised to defend his honor.

"I'd bet a month's wages on it."

"Ma would skin us alive if we took to betting, so you count yourself blessed with a month's wages you'd have otherwise lost."

Jack slapped him on the back and laughed. "You have a good mind, little brother."

Dell glared them to silence, then turned to Emily. "The kiss isn't necessarily the point, Em, although I'm a bit disappointed to see you kissing a man you're not willing to marry. The point is that your virtue has been compromised despite your claims of innocence. If one of your brothers spent three days alone with a young lady, whether he kissed her or not, I'd expect him to do the decent thing and marry her."

Jeremiah stepped forward. "Emily, take some time to think about the repercussions of not making this right."

"There's nothing to make right. I've done nothing wrong, and I refuse to get married just to satisfy a town full of people who delight in thinking the worst."

"You're just being stubborn." He gripped her upper arm and drew her close. "No one can kiss a man the way you kissed me—forgive me for bringing it up, Mr. St. John—no one can kiss a man the way you did if she doesn't care something for him."

Emily's face glowed, but she lifted her chin and held herself with dignity. "Don't be so conceited."

"Have it your way." Jeremiah released her arm. "But I won't ask again."

"Now, don't be too hasty." Mr. St. John stepped forward and pulled Emily close to his side. "After a few days at the ranch with your family, maybe you'll see things a bit more clearly."

"I see things clearly enough, thank you. My mind's made up. Pa, please give Ma my love and assure her I'm fine, but I can't go to the ranch and leave my store any more days. Why, Jeremiah will get all my customers."

Dell chuckled. "I suppose you have a point there." He gathered a breath and shrugged, sending Jeremiah an apologetic look. "Looks like there won't be a wedding, after all. I might be a bit old-fashioned, but not so much so that I'd force an unwanted marriage on my daughter. We'll find some way to make it through this. Come on, Sweetheart. I'll take you home and help you get settled back into your room."

"It's only across the street. I can make it."

The relief on Emily's face was downright insulting.

Dell sent his irate daughter a smirk. "The snow is two feet deep through town and higher in drifts, Honey. Maybe you better let me take you home in the sleigh."

She pinkened and gave a short nod. "Fine, then."

Jeremiah's ire rose as she looked ready to leave without so much as a good-bye. "Hold on a minute. I want it made clear that this decision is not a result of my refusal to marry you. You might not care about your reputation in this town, Emily, but I won't have my mother humiliated."

Emily's eyes narrowed. "Rest assured, I will take full responsibility for not getting married. The talebearers of this town will be made aware of the truth. And if any other story emerges, painting you in a bad light, I'll take out an advertisement in Mr. Bell's newspaper."

So saying, she swung around and stomped to the door. Her brothers made a path through the doorway. Jeremiah followed her and watched as Luke swooped her up in his arms and waded waist deep in the snow until he reached the sleigh.

"Good-bye, Jeremiah," Emily said, once she was settled. "Th–Thank you for everything. Send me a bill for my portion of the supplies we used up and for this coat."

Too angry to speak, Jeremiah closed the door without even saying good-bye.

Emily might think that was the end of it, but she was sorely mistaken. She had lived all of her life with people's approval if for no other reason than because she was a St. John. But he'd worked too hard to gain a little respectability, and he refused to be made a fool of in his own town.

Jeremiah walked to the counter and started to straighten up. A grin split his face at a sudden thought. After a few days of enduring the town's displeasure, she'd be ready to accept his proposal.

ten

Emily was amazed at how quickly word spread. The forthcoming scandal weighed heavily on her mind, but she couldn't help but be secretly thrilled with all the business the town's curiosity generated for Emily's Place. Jeremiah's also seemed to be teeming with customers. Emily was glad, for Jeremiah's sake.

Two weeks had passed since the snow had ceased to fall, and business had been practically nonexistent until the past couple of days. But now, folks were slowly digging out of their homes and coming into town for supplies. Already she'd practically sold out of household essentials such as lard and flour. Hopefully, the supply train would be able to get through soon.

She smiled at Mrs. McDonald. "Would you like that to go on account, Ma'am?"

"Yes, Dear." The woman turned to her husband. "Take these out to the wagon, Rafe. I'll be along directly."

"Don't be all day about it, Woman," he said gruffly, but Emily noted he took the crate of supplies and moved through the door.

Mrs. McDonald turned back to Emily, a look of expectation plainly written on her lined face.

"Do you need anything else?" Emily asked, steeling herself for what would most certainly be the question on everyone's mind.

Pink tinged the matron's cheeks. "I—well. . .I don't mean to pry, but I am curious about the wedding."

"Wedding?" Emily glanced at the counter and brushed away an imaginary speck of dust. "Do you mean Lionel's wedding? I thought your son wasn't getting married until spring."

"No, Dear. I'm speaking of you and Jeremiah Daniels, of

course. If you don't make an announcement soon, folks won't have an opportunity to get you gifts."

Emily released a sigh. "I appreciate the concern, but Jeremiah and I aren't getting married."

Mrs. McDonald fingered the cameo brooch at her neck. "Oh, my. You mean Jeremiah's playing the cad? I never would have thought it of him. True, he started out a bit rough in his boyhood days, but he appeared to straighten right up once Tuck hired him." She shook her head and clucked her tongue. "Don't you worry. I will speak to Mrs. Daniels about him. She'll put him in his place real quick like. You'll be a married woman before you know it."

Emily knew the only fair thing to do was to explain the truth of the situation. This would only be the beginning of the gossip. But for Jeremiah's sake, she had to be honest. "To tell you the truth, he proposed immediately."

Confusion clouded the older woman's blue eyes. "Well, then—"

"I turned him down."

"You turned him down?"

"Yes, Ma'am."

"But why?"

"Because I felt it was the right thing to do. Jeremiah and I did nothing wrong. I see no reason we should have to get married."

A look of understanding suddenly replaced the woman's confusion. "I'd forgotten you hold to all these newfangled ideas about votes for women and whatnot. Times sure are changing, and I'm not altogether convinced it's for the best. Not that I am opposed to a woman having a little independence, mind you."

The middle-aged matron leaned in close and dropped her volume. She patted Emily's hand. "But don't you think you ought to snatch him up while you have the chance, Honey? I doubt you'll get a better offer, what with my Lionel spoken for."

Heat suffused Emily's cheeks as her anger rose. She had half a mind to inform the nosy matron she wouldn't take Lionel if he were delivered on a silver platter. Catching her tongue just before blurting out the truth of the matter, she addressed the issue at hand. "No, Ma'am, I do not feel I should 'snatch up' anyone."

Customers turned in curiosity at the rise in Emily's tone. She glanced helplessly around, then made a split-second decision. "While I have everyone's attention, I'd like to make an announcement." All murmuring ceased, and the store grew as still as closing time.

"All right, then." Emily took in the fifteen customers in one sweeping glance. "First, let me say that Jeremiah Daniels is as fine a gentleman as Harper has ever seen."

Sudden, knowing grins split the faces staring back at her.

"However," Emily forged ahead, "I will not be marrying him, so you can all just stop wondering when the wedding will take place."

Looks of outrage replaced the humor. Emily held up her hand. "As I was just telling Mrs. McDonald, this decision is not Jeremiah's doing. He asked me to marry him. The choice not to do so is mine."

Her patrons stood, no one speaking or moving until finally Mr. Gregory made his way forward from the back of the room. His wife trailed behind him, her head lowered.

He stared at Emily, eyes glinting hard. The family had moved into the area only weeks before Christmas, but Emily had rarely seen any of them. Mr. Gregory had bought the local hotel, immediately closing the dance hall beneath.

According to Amelia Bell, the man had wasted no time setting his wife and five daughters to work cleaning every corner and crack of the place. His plans were to add more hotel rooms below, take away the gaudy remnants of the former, disreputable business, and make it a respectable hotel.

The League of Christian Women, which had been trying

to close the dance hall since it opened, had embraced the new family with open arms.

Standing before the disapproving gaze of the stone-faced giant of a man, Emily shook, thoroughly intimidated.

"And why is it that you would refuse a man who is only trying to do the right thing by you?" he asked, his voice gruff, his manner bordering on hostile.

Fearing her wobbly legs might not keep her upright, Emily gripped the edge of the counter so tightly her knuckles grew white. She averted her gaze and found Mrs. Thomas—who had recently taken to wearing bloomer outfits almost exclusively—staring at her. The fellow suffragette nodded her support, bolstering Emily's resolve.

She squared her shoulders and looked way up to meet his gaze head on. "Because, Sir, I don't feel that any woman, or man for that matter, should be forced into doing something just to satisfy the expectations of others."

A sneer marred his face. "Is that right?"

Emily felt her burst of courage failing beneath his condemning gaze. She stared, unable to find the appropriate words, and squirmed uncomfortably at his sardonic smile. "Can't think of anything to say? Let me tell you something, Miss St. John. Women like you are an infection on society."

A gasp flew from Emily's lips. She pressed her palm to her chest.

"That's right. You break down the structure of decent homes and spread your lies to unsuspecting, weak-minded women who don't know any better than to believe they are just as good as the men who provide for them. I'd strongly advise you not to go near my wife and daughters if you know what's good for you."

Quick, booted steps on the wooden floor marked the end to Mrs. Thomas's patience. "Now, see here, you big fool of a man. This girl happens to be the daughter of one of Harper's most celebrated citizens. You would do well not to threaten her if you know what's good for you."

Apparently undaunted, he swept Mrs. Thomas with a dismissive gaze. "I am well aware of Miss St. John's family status. Her activities reflect poorly on her family. Even as a new member of this community, I have to wonder what her pa is thinking by allowing her to run a business and live alone in the first place. She would never have been compromised if she had stayed properly at home under her father's care, where she belongs."

At the criticism of her family, Emily found her tongue. "H—How dare you suggest my pa doesn't do right by me!"

The man's lips twitched in a smile that didn't come near his eyes. "I am only stating the obvious. Your pa clearly can't manage a proper household."

"Why, why you get out of my store this instant. I—I, you are not welcome here again."

"You forget, Miss, I am a customer, and I have supplies I'd like to buy."

"That's too bad. I'll not sell you a thing."

His face reddened in anger, and his nostrils flared. "Come, now. These items are not to be had across the street. And despite your lack of concern for Mr. Daniels's reputation, he has graciously sent me to your place of business."

"Mr. Gregory, I don't care if you can't buy flour or rice or chickpeas anywhere else. I will not do business with a man who holds me in such poor regard that he would stand in my store and insult my family and my honor right to my face." She waved toward the other customers, who stared in bewilderment at the exchange. "Especially in the presence of so many others. Please leave, and kindly do not return."

From the corner of her eye, Emily noted movement from Mrs. Gregory, who thus far had not looked up. She did so now, throwing a cautious glance to the back of her husband's head, and then fleetingly met Emily's gaze. Mrs. Gregory held her gaze for only a second, but Emily noted the look of admiration shining from her eyes.

Mr. Gregory's cold hand gripped Emily's, drawing her attention back to him. "I'm afraid you didn't hear me correctly. I will purchase these items, or I will take them without purchasing them. It's really your choice."

Shaking with rage, Emily found all the courage she needed. She jerked her hand from his and, with a quick sweep of her arm, she cleared the counter of Mr. Gregory's purchases, sending them to the floor at her feet. "No! I will not be bullied, Sir. It's really your choice. You may leave, or I'll send for the sheriff. I have a right to refuse service to anyone I choose. And I choose not to serve you."

"I think it's about time you leave, Mr. Gregory."

Intent on the situation at hand, Emily hadn't even noticed the bell above the door ding Jeremiah's entrance. He stood at the threshold. Emily's heart pounded at the sight of him standing poised to defend her if necessary. Relief flooded her, and she willed herself not to burst into tears.

Mr. Gregory looked from Jeremiah, then back to Emily. He sneered and leaned easily across the counter. "You just made yourself an enemy, Miss."

In a flash, Jeremiah stood at his side. He grabbed Mr. Gregory's arm and jerked him upright. "Don't threaten her. Ever."

A short laugh emanated from deep inside the burly man. "Are you going to ban me from your store as well?"

"No, Sir. I'll take your money anytime you feel the need to spend it. I'm just telling you to leave Emily alone."

"You'd defend her after she's made a fool of you?"

"I'd defend anyone against the likes of you."

"I'll be taking my business to Henderson's from now on. I'd rather drive ten miles for supplies than to patronize either of your stores." He grabbed his wife by her upper arm and pulled her out of the store. Emily watched in astonishment as he practically dragged her down the steps and down the street to the hotel. Never in her twenty-five years had she seen a woman treated in such a manner.

"Oh, Jeremiah."

"I know," he said grimly. "Men like that don't deserve to have families."

"And he had the audacity to criticize the way my pa runs our household."

"Are you all right?" He covered her hand.

The warmth brought an immediate end to her trembling. Keenly aware of the remaining customers' watchful observation, Emily gathered a shaky breath and nodded. She slid her hand out from his. "Thank you for your assistance, Jeremiah."

He glanced cautiously about. "I best get back across the street. I left the store in Ma's hands." A grin split his face. "She'll be raising prices if I don't keep an eye on her."

"Your ma's helping out in the store?"

He sent her a wink and leaned in closer. "She's afraid it might storm, and I might get stranded with you again."

Emily's eyes widened until she noted the teasing glint in his eyes.

He smiled. "She was going stir crazy after the last two weeks of being cooped up at home, so I asked her if she'd like to come to town. She spent the morning at an impromptu sewing circle with some of the town women." He cast an apologetic look at Mrs. Thomas, who at least pretended to be studying a bottle of Healy's Magic Elixir, unlike the rest of the onlookers, who stared unabashed.

Giving up all pretense of not eavesdropping, Mrs. Thomas smiled broadly. "Don't worry about my not being invited to their little sewing circle, Mr. Daniels. I wouldn't want to attend anyway." She turned her attention to Emily. "I must be going, Dear." Now it was her turn to send a cautious glance at Jeremiah. "Don't bend to society's antiquated opinions. Keep to your convictions. The movement is firmly behind you." She hurried to the door and raised her fist in salute. "Votes for women!"

Emily returned her gaze to Jeremiah's. He cleared his throat. "I guess that's that. I'll talk to you later, Emily." He lifted his hand in farewell to their audience. "You folks have a good day, and keep in mind you'll find a better deal at Jeremiah's."

Emily's mouth dropped open. "That's not true! I'll beat his prices any day."

His laughter followed him down the mercantile steps.

That was the most spiteful thing she'd ever heard of! Trying to steal her customers just because she wouldn't marry him. She was glad she'd said no.

But as she tallied Mrs. Adams's purchases, Emily faced the truth. She deeply regretted her hasty decision. Jeremiah had made it clear he wouldn't ask her again, and she felt helpless to right this dreadful wrong. One by one, she took care of her customers, speaking only as was necessary to conclude their business.

She watched the last of her patrons leave and close the door. Releasing a heavy sigh, she bent and began cleaning the mess she'd made.

It was one thing when she, alone, was bearing the brunt of the talk; but if her family had to suffer because of her decision, Emily knew she couldn't live with that. She understood now why Jeremiah had considered his mother's standing in town. Her decision was causing negative repercussions for both families.

She glanced out of the window to Jeremiah's. Jeremiah and his mother exited the store together. Mrs. Daniels waited while he locked the door; then with a grin, he turned and offered her his arm.

Mrs. Taylor, the mayor's wife, walked past with only the slightest of nods. Emily seethed at the deliberate snub. Her heart lurched as Mrs. Daniels watched the mayor's wife until Jeremiah tugged at her. With a nod, they headed toward the livery.

Tears stung Emily's eyes. *They don't deserve this scandal, Lord. How do I make it right?*

Without taking the time to grab a jacket, Emily sprinted to the door, flung it open, and stepped out onto the stoop. "Jeremiah, wait!"

eleven

"Don't turn around, Son. Just keep walking."

"That wouldn't be very polite." Jeremiah chuckled as he watched Emily race down the steps and pause to allow a wagon to pass. "Where are those fine manners I've always admired in you, Ma?"

Ma snorted in a rather rude fashion. "Where are her manners? That girl made a spectacle of you and then refused your proposal as though she's too good to marry a Daniels."

Jeremiah had thought the same thing more than once when his wounded pride got the better of him. Still, he couldn't very well pretend not to hear her when everyone in town was staring.

Especially when she'd already caught up to them. She stood scowling and red-faced. "Honestly, Jeremiah, you might have stopped and met me halfway," Emily said, pressing her hand flat against her stomach as she tried to catch her breath.

"You should be glad he stopped at all, young lady!" Ma huffed, shaking her plump finger at Emily.

"Indeed?" Emily's eyes narrowed to slits, and she looked like a tabby cat about to spit and claw.

Ma wasn't acting much better as she coiled like a rattler in the barnyard. Jeremiah stepped between them before she could strike. "Ma, would you go on over to the livery and ask Mr. Collins if he'd mind hitching the team?"

Ma harrumphed and set off without another word.

Emily watched her stomp away. "I guess she's a little mad at me, huh?"

"A little," Jeremiah said wryly.

"I am sorry, Jeremiah. You were right. Our families are

going to suffer from this if we don't get married."

Jeremiah took her by the arm and pulled her out of the way of a curious matron walking by on the wooden sidewalk. "What are you saying?"

Emily's face grew red. "I just. . .I know you said you wouldn't ask again, and I don't blame you. So. . .well, I guess I'll have to ask you to do the honorable thing and marry me after all." She glanced at him, hesitating briefly as if to gauge his reaction. Worry clouded her eyes, giving Jeremiah the satisfaction of knowing his feigned nonchalance appeared to be convincing.

"Now you want to marry me?"

A frown creased her brow. "This is for our families. After Mr. Gregory's comments in there. . . He. . .well, Jeremiah, he insulted my pa because of me."

"I see." Jeremiah knew all it would take to alleviate her discomfort was to reassure her everything would be all right and that of course he'd marry her; but the fact was, he rather enjoyed seeing her grovel after what she'd put him through during the past two weeks.

She nodded. "A—and when he insulted my pa, I understood what you meant about your ma having to withstand the town's disapproval. Don't you see? I realized us getting married is. . .it's just the right thing to do. For their sakes."

Jeremiah leaned against the wall and folded his arms across his chest. He regarded her evenly. "What if I don't think it's necessary, anymore? Everyone knows I was perfectly willing to do the honorable thing by you. And if they don't, they will by the end of the week. After all, you just made an announcement in Emily's Place that you weren't marrying me even though I proposed."

Emily frowned, clearly perplexed. "How did you know about that? You didn't come in the store until later."

"Mrs. McDonald came to Jeremiah's to buy eggs since you were out. She told me all about it. Said you spoke very highly of me. . .even called me a 'fine gentleman'." Jeremiah sent her a sardonic grin and shrugged. "I think my reputation is pretty much secure. So you see, marriage isn't really necessary, after all. Not for me, anyway."

Emily's eyes widened and her lips tightened. "You can't just take back a proposal! Once you ask, it's out there waiting to be answered."

"But you forget, Miss St. John. My proposal was already answered. With a resounding no."

She brought her foot down hard on the sidewalk. "And now I'm taking it back. My answer is yes."

He moved away from the wall and headed toward the livery. "I'll have to think about it."

"You'll have to what?"

"I said," he called over his shoulder, "I'll have to think about it. I'll let you know soon."

"Why, you. . ." Her boots clacked on the sidewalk behind him as she hurried to catch up. Jeremiah grinned to himself.

Emily stepped quickly to keep up with his long strides. "I'll—yes—I will, I'll have my brothers after you, and my pa," she caught her breath, "and every ranch hand working on Pa's ranch and my brother Luke's ranch."

Jeremiah shrugged and kept walking. "You can have all those men come after me if you want, but I figure your pa can handle me without anyone's help—even if he is twice my age. I'm not really much of a fighter." Halting, he turned to her, unable to keep the smile at bay any longer. "Emily, thank you for reconsidering. Let's get married."

Outrage flooded Emily's face. She opened her mouth, closed it, then put her hands on her hips. "You were only teasing? You put me through all that when you had every intention of marrying me all along?"

"Well, not all along. For the first couple of seconds, I considered turning you down; but you wooed me so sweetly, I found myself unable to resist."

Obviously not amused, Emily narrowed her eyes. "If my family honor weren't at stake, I'd change my mind!"

"Again?"

"Yes, again!" She glared at him, then hesitated before asking, "When do you want to get married?"

The sudden question surprised Jeremiah. He sobered. "I don't know. Now?"

"Now?" The look Emily gave him spoke volumes, but Jeremiah didn't figure there were any flattering words to describe him. "I can't get ready for a wedding in two minutes."

"Why don't you just decide when the happy event will take place, then?"

"All right, I will."

Jeremiah tipped his bowler and headed back toward the livery. "Let me know when to show up, and I'll be there in my Sunday best," he called over his shoulder.

"Jeremiah?"

At the softening in her tone, Jeremiah turned. "Yes?"

"I. . .just. . ." She shook her head. "Nothing. I'll speak with my family and contact you in a couple of days."

"I'll look forward to hearing from you."

Her lips tipped upward in a tentative smile. She looked about to turn around, then stopped. "You won't be sorry. I promise." And without waiting for his reply, she spun around and hurried back to the mercantile.

Jeremiah swallowed hard. If only she'd given him a chance to voice the words his heart sang. *I could never be sorry for marrying the girl of my dreams.*

❧

Amelia Bell's grinning, elflike face greeted Emily as she walked through the door, breathless from her sprint across the street and up the steps.

"So you were talking to Jeremiah?" The lilt in the reporter's voice sent a shiver of annoyance down Emily's spine.

"Do you need something, Amelia?" Emily walked to the

counter and gave her a pointed look. "I mean something other than information?"

Undaunted, Amelia crossed the room as well. She leaned against the counter. "No. Living in town has its advantages. We didn't run out of everything and have to restock like most of the township."

Grabbing a cloth from beneath the counter, Emily swiped at imaginary dust. "Then, if you'll excuse me, I have work to do."

"Gracious, I had no idea all the hoopla stealing a little sugar would cause. It's been great for town gossip, though."

Emily's mouth went suddenly dry. "What do you mean?"

An impish grin split Amelia's face. "You two were getting altogether too chummy and providing me with nothing of interest to report. Harper is a very dull town for news, you know. Other than your brother and Laney having a baby, nothing has happened in months."

"Are you telling me you staged the robbery? Whatever for?" Emily's insides ached. All of this could have been avoided. "Was it a trick?"

"Newspaper sales doubled when I started writing about you and Jeremiah's war between the stores. Then Jeremiah got a lovesick look in his eyes and was offering you half his stock. No one wants to read 'Jeremiah's bails out Emily's Place— Proprietor offers half of sugar stock.' "

"Amelia Bell, I've half a mind to go straight to the sheriff."

Amelia shrugged. "Go ahead. At least if he made an arrest I'd have a story to report."

Emily scowled. "You're hopeless. Do you realize all the trouble you've caused? Jeremiah is forced into marrying me because of you."

Victory washed across Amelia's features. "So that's what you were discussing. You've decided to marry him after all. I guess after Mr. Gregory's little outburst, you really don't have a choice. Can't have Mr. St. John's name besmirched, can we?"

"How did you know about Mr. Gregory?" Did the folks in

Harper have nothing else to do but report on the goings-on at her mercantile?

"I have my sources." She grinned. "So, when's the wedding?"

Emily released a defeated sigh. "I don't know yet. Pa's coming in tomorrow night to take me to the ranch. I suppose I'll discuss everything with him and Ma at supper."

"You will let me know, right?"

"Are you going to print it in the paper?"

"Of course. Folks will want to know. You gave us our first bona fide scandal since you bought this store and joined the cause."

"Actually, you gave us this scandal with your little sugar stunt."

"You're right. I guess I owe myself a reward." She took a penny from her reticule and slapped it down on the counter. "I believe I'd fancy a licorice stick."

Emily smiled despite her irritation. Amelia was like an ornery child at times. It was almost impossible to stay angry with the nosy little woman.

"Mrs. Thomas is going to be disappointed," Amelia said with a mouthful of candy.

"What do you mean?"

"That you're marrying Jeremiah, of course."

Emily stared blankly.

"Oh, Emily, sometimes you're too naïve for your own good." Amelia's laughter filled the air. "Surely you know you've given Mrs. Thomas something to bolster Harper's chapter of the Association?"

"I've no idea what you're talking about." Emily sniffed, pretending she didn't care to discuss it. Still, she was relieved when Amelia continued.

"There were only a handful of women interested in the movement when Mrs. Thomas introduced it a couple of years ago. Five or six at the most, and those were matrons whom everyone already knew bullied their husbands. With only a handful of battleaxes to their credit, the group lacked credibility with most of the women in Harper—especially the young, unmarried women with high hopes for matrimony.

"But when you bought this store and the League of Christian Women voiced their outrage at a woman being in business for herself, why Mrs. Thomas took up your righteous cause. She immediately became your champion, and it was quite selfless of her. Within a month, our local chapter tripled in size and continued to grow despite the efforts of Jeremiah's mother and her fellow Christian Leaguers."

"But what did I have to do with that?"

"Darling. . . With a pretty young face in the crowd, the suffragettes were finally viewed as more than dried-up sour-faced dowagers with nothing to do but cause trouble and make their husbands sorry they'd been born. I'd have never joined the cause myself if it hadn't been for you."

"So Mrs. Thomas used me."

"Yep, just like I used you to sell papers." She grinned. "You're an easy target because you're a St. John. People are interested in your family. You're the royal family of Harper."

Emily couldn't help but laugh. "Don't you think you're exaggerating a bit?"

"Not really. Your brother Sam is the doctor, Luke has the second largest ranch in the area—second only to your pa's ranch—your oldest sister is married to the preacher, Jack is studying law, Will is the most popular male among all the young people in town, Hope has an absolute entourage of boys and girls alike, and little Cat isn't far behind. I hear she is top of her class at school and sings beautifully enough to be on the stage. And then there's you."

Yes, then there was her. Listening to Amelia regale the attributes of her family members, Emily once again felt the weight of inferiority. "Let's don't talk about me."

"Why not? You're the St. Johniest of all the St. Johns, Princess Emily."

Emily bit back a grin, not wanting to encourage her ridiculous notions. "I haven't the faintest idea what you mean."

"You, my dear, are making your own way in the world. . . defying the odds of a patriarchal society, firm in your determination to keep yourself free of the domination of a man."

She sounded as though she were formulating a headline. Emily hated to be the one to bring her back to reality, particularly when the subject was rather flattering. However. . .

"You forget. My marriage is imminent."

"Oh, that's right." Amelia gave a troubled sigh. "I suppose it is my own fault for getting you compromised."

"You see what your meddling ways caused?"

"In any case, Mrs. Thomas will be fit to be tied unless you find a way to make it appear you're getting everything you want out of the marriage."

"What do you mean?" What did anyone want from marriage? A home. Love. Children, eventually. Emily's mind conjured the image of holding a child in her arms. She smiled.

"All right, you'll have to get rid of the dreamy look on your face or we'll never appease Mrs. Thomas—unless you don't care about losing her support. Are you ready to join the ranks of the rest of the mousy housewives in Harper who have no say-so in how they live?"

Emily thought about it for a moment. Amelia was right. The store and the cause were her only achievements that meant anything. She wasn't beautiful, extra smart, or talented like her siblings. All she had was Emily's Place, and the only women who understood her were Mrs. Thomas and the women she led as they fought for their civil liberties. If she let them go, she'd be back where she started a year ago. . .nobody.

Gathering a deep breath, she leveled her gaze at Amelia. "All right. What do we do?"

Amelia smiled. "Let's get to work on a plan of action that insures you don't have to give up any of your independence. You can present it to Jeremiah before the wedding, and we can assure Mrs. Thomas that you haven't compromised your ideals one bit by marrying Jeremiah, after all."

Niggles of doubt twisted through Emily, but she quickly dismissed it. This was the way it had to be. If she hadn't over-heard Jeremiah and Harold talking the night of the harvest dance, she might not have agreed to Amelia's bold plan. But as it was, she was taking measures to insure she never had to give up her store.

twelve

Jeremiah scratched the back of his leg with the toe of his boot while he nervously waited for Emily to arrive at the church. His mother sat, dressed in her darkest blue dress and dabbing at her nose with a lacy handkerchief. She would have pulled her mourning clothes from mothballs had Jeremiah not threatened to leave her home if she even tried.

He knew she worried. But many marriages began only for convenience, he'd reminded her, and most were successful. He intended for his marriage to be in the latter category. The fact that he loved his bride could only help to ease the situation. Without being too immodest, he believed Emily cared for him as well. Their shared kiss just before her pa had arrived after the blizzard had been a hopeful indication of that.

He glanced about the room and met the questioning glances of the guests waiting for the ceremony to begin. The suffragettes had turned out to the affair, and Mrs. Thomas even cast off her bloomer outfit in favor of an appropriate green satin gown, although her mouth was twisted, making her disapproval abundantly clear.

The St. John family took two benches on the other side of the church, and the townsfolk filled the rest of the seats. Now if only the bride would show up, the wedding could commence. Jeremiah pulled at his tight collar and cleared his throat.

"Don't worry." Anthony gave him an understanding smile. "Tarah and her ma are helping Emily dress at the parsonage. She'll be here."

"She's a half hour late," Jeremiah growled. "Sorry, Reverend."

Anthony clapped him on the shoulder and chuckled. "I was

a young groom once, myself. Wedding lateness seems to be a female tradition in this family. From what I understand, not one of them, beginning with Mrs. St. John, has been on time yet. So think of this as a good sign."

"A good sign of what?"

A chuckle rumbled in the reverend's chest. "I have no idea. I was just trying to make you feel better."

"Psst."

"What was that?" Jeremiah asked.

Anthony shrugged.

The two men glanced about.

"Psst."

The sound definitely wasn't coming from the guests. Anthony nudged him and gestured toward the back door. Jeremiah turned. He saw Emily's head and face through an opening only wide enough for her to get his attention. His heart plummeted. Surely she wouldn't call things off now that everyone in town had shown up for the service.

She motioned to him. Amid twitters of laughter, Jeremiah strode to the door, the clack of his boots incredibly loud on the wooden planks. He stepped outside and closed the door behind him, then stopped short and gaped.

The sight of Emily dressed in a gown of white silk hit him like a punch in the gut. A matching white ribbon woven through her braided hair added regal appeal to her already breathtaking beauty. Her chin lifted with an air of dignity, which only heightened the effect of her hair, twisted in layers atop her head. Emily St. John looked like a queen. The honor of becoming her husband shot through Jeremiah, and suddenly he felt kingly himself.

"Are you all right?" she asked, pulling him from his stupor.

Ears burning, he cleared his throat and smiled. "You're beautiful." Bending at the waist, he kissed her cheek, forcing back the desire to take her into his arms and claim those full, soft lips.

"Oh, Jeremiah." Her voice almost seemed to hold a moan beneath the words.

A sense of dread slithered through Jeremiah. He steeled himself against what was coming, determined not to show his anxiety.

"What's the holdup, Emily? We have a church full of guests back there."

From the corner of his eye, he caught movement and cut a glance in that direction. For the first time since stepping outside, he noticed Tarah and Cassidy standing a few feet away, both faces clouded with worry.

Looking from one woman to the next, he scowled, sensing a conspiracy. He focused his gaze on his lovely fiancée. "Are we getting married or not?"

Emily cleared her throat. "That depends entirely upon you."

"Good. Then let's go." Jeremiah snatched her hand and headed back toward the door.

"Wait!"

Somehow, he had known it wouldn't be that easy. He halted and turned to face her. Concern washed over him. Her face had gone white as the church house. Instead of releasing her as he'd planned, he pulled her close, pressing their clasped hands against his chest. "What's on your mind?"

Cassidy cleared her throat loudly. "You two certainly don't need us." She held out a document to Emily. "Here you are, Sweetheart."

"Are you sure about this, Em?" Tarah asked. "It would be better if you just tear it up."

Emily pulled away from Jeremiah's steady grasp. "I'm sure."

Cassidy stepped forward and gave her a quick hug. "Then I guess we'll run along and wait with the rest of the family and your guests."

Cassidy beat a hasty exit, followed closely by Tarah.

With a raised brow, Jeremiah met Emily's gaze. "I suppose you're going to tell me what that is."

Emily dropped her gaze and unfolded the paper. "Yes. It's a contract of sorts. Between the two of us."

"I thought the marriage certificate was a contract."

"It is. As far as the legality of our actual marriage is concerned. But this. . . Here, just go ahead and read it for yourself."

Jeremiah saw the print, read the words, and still couldn't believe what they conveyed. "You expect me to sign this?" he asked incredulously.

"Yes. Before we say our vows. I have to protect my interests."

"Your interests? I thought they would be our interests once we're married."

"I want your word you'll allow me to continue to operate Emily's Place as I see fit. That you won't go behind my back and try to sell it or try to force me to stay home and cook and clean while you take over both stores."

"Why would I want to do that? I have my hands full with one. Besides, legally, your property is yours. Didn't you know that?"

"Yes, but that doesn't stop men from taking over or bullying their wives into giving up what they own."

"Don't you trust me?" Pain knifed through Jeremiah. If she didn't trust him, she couldn't love him.

"Will you sign?"

Jeremiah had hoped to merge the two stores and run them together with Emily as his partner. Now, to even mention it would cause her to think he wanted to steal from her. He steeled his heart against the pain and leveled his gaze at her. "You're sure you want to do this like a business arrangement rather than a marriage?"

"I'm sure." Her lips pressed together in a grim line.

"All right. I'll sign. For one reason only—if we call off the wedding now, it will cause more of a scandal than it would if you had just kept your original plan not to marry me."

"I understand."

Her grim, businesslike attitude sent a tremor of annoyance

through him. Emily had made her position abundantly clear. Fine, he'd play her game, though he inwardly cringed, knowing playing games with the holy institution of marriage was a dangerous thing. Still how could he agree to her terms and expect to have an honest relationship? Until she trusted him, they'd have to keep things at a business level. He gathered a deep breath. "Another thing. . . Once I sign the contract, promising to leave Emily's Place firmly in your care, we enter into a business arrangement—not a marriage."

Emily's eyes grew wide. "What do you mean?"

"Exactly what you think I mean. You'll live at my farm because it would cause too much talk otherwise, but we won't pretend at marriage. This is for appearances only and to protect our families from scandal. That's what you wanted, right? My ma will be the only person aware of our living arrangements, and I assure you she won't reveal it to anyone."

"For appearances only? But what about. . ." Emily's face reddened.

"What? Children?"

She nodded and ducked her head.

Jeremiah sneered. "Why do you need children? You'll be too busy running Emily's Place to take care of them. Or do you plan to hold a baby while you measure dress goods and make change?"

"Well, you don't have to be insulting! All I am asking for is a little respect for my rights as a businesswoman."

"Insulting? Honey, this contract is an insult. All you had to do was ask me to stay out of your business and let you run it and I would have. Instead you accuse me of being underhanded. If you had given me the chance, I would have told you how proud I am to have a wife to share my business with—someone I can talk things over with who will understand all the ins and outs of owning a mercantile. I looked forward to the end of the day to sharing that with you."

"But, Jeremiah, we can still—"

"No, you want us to stay competitors. So decide. Right now. Either I sign the contract, and we enter into a business agreement; or I don't, and we join our lives in every way. I won't force you, but you can't have it both ways. A man can only take so much."

Jeremiah held his breath and studied the struggle of emotions crossing her face. His hopes dashed to the ground when she squared her shoulders and met his gaze evenly.

He motioned toward the parsonage. "Let's go and sign this so we can get on with it. The good people of Harper don't want to wait all day to watch the most anticipated wedding of the year."

⬥

Emily squinted against the blinding sunset. The wagon rattled, the only sound breaking the thick silence around Emily, Jeremiah, and Mrs. Daniels as they made their way toward the Danielses' farm.

Emily Daniels. Emily Daniels. She'd been trying on the name all day, though she hadn't quite had the nerve to speak it aloud. Heaviness covered her like a thick, suffocating quilt—not the freedom she'd expected to feel over her victory.

Jeremiah had signed the contract in the parsonage and headed back to the church, leaving her with no option but to follow. Somehow, she had the feeling she'd made the biggest mistake of her life—not in marrying Jeremiah, but in insisting he sign a contract between them.

She shot a sideways glance and caught a glimpse of her husband's tightly clenched square jaw. His shoulders rose and fell as he stared intently at the rutted ground ahead of them, carefully maneuvering the horses around the worst of the dips and holes.

He turned his head and slowly met her gaze. Rather than condemnation, anger, accusation, or any of the emotions Emily would have expected to find flashing in his eyes, she was taken aback by the smile he gave her. Her throat tightened, and her eyes stung with unshed tears. She would do anything if given the chance to go back a few hours and tear up that hateful contract.

The wagon suddenly lurched, pulling Jeremiah's attention back to the road, the last stretch leading up to the Danielses' farm.

"Well, we're home," Mrs. Daniels said matter-of-factly. Emily could feel Jeremiah's gaze upon her as she studied her new home. The dwelling was made of sandstone like her pa's ranch house. Only this house was very small in comparison. She imagined there was only one bedroom and maybe a loft.

Emily's heart leapt, and she pictured children running about the yard, chasing squawking hens and feeding the hogs penned up next to the barn. She could see a miniature Jeremiah or two and a couple of redheaded girls following after her as she took apple cider to her hard-working husband.

Mrs. Daniels cleared her throat loudly, arresting Emily's attention. Heat crept to her cheeks as she realized she was the only one left on the wagon seat and Jeremiah stood waiting to help her down.

"Sorry," she muttered.

The older woman harrumphed and stomped to the house.

"It's not much after what you grew up living in, I know." Jeremiah lifted her down, then turned to the back of the wagon and started to grab her things.

"Not at all, Jeremiah. It's lovely. W—will you be building a home for us, or. . ."

"Ma stays with us until the house and land pass to me," he said, a note of finality edging his tone. With her bag in hand, he brushed past, sweeping her a sideways glance. "It's not like we're going to need more room, is it?"

When they entered the house, Mrs. Daniels already stood before the cookstove, stoking the coals. "All that waiting at the church killed the fire," she grumbled. "I'm going to have to build it back up before I can start supper."

Emily's face warmed. "I'm sorry, Mrs. Daniels," she said. "May I help?"

The woman turned on her. "I won't have you soiling your fancy clothes," she huffed. "Get yourself settled in. Supper will be ready in a couple of hours."

"Come with me, Emily," Jeremiah said. "I'll show you where you'll sleep."

Following meekly, Emily could feel her mother-in-law's gaze burning into her back. She squared her shoulders and trailed after Jeremiah across the room and into the only separate room from the rest of the house.

Inside, a lovely four-poster bed sat against the far wall, displaying a rose-covered quilt. "Your ma thought you might like to have that."

Emily strode to the bed and sat. She smoothed her fingertips over the soft quilt, picturing it on Pa's and Ma's bed for as long as she could remember. "Yes, I've always loved this quilt. Ma promised me years ago that it would be mine on my wedding day. I'd forgotten."

"I'll leave you to start unpacking while I unload the rest of your things. Where do you want your rocking chair?"

"How about in front of the fireplace for cold evenings? Ma and Pa always sit and talk before a fire."

"I'm sorry, Emily. There isn't a fireplace. Pa always said they were a waste of wood. And in these parts we couldn't afford to waste any."

"That sounds reasonable." She sighed and waved. "I suppose it doesn't matter, then. Anywhere your ma would like for it to go is fine with me."

With a frown, Jeremiah closed the distance between them and sat next to her. "Things aren't going to be easy for any of us, but I want you to think of this as your home too."

"There's only one bedroom," she said flatly. "Where is your mother going to sleep? She can't really climb into the loft at her age, can she?"

Jeremiah chuckled. "You probably didn't notice, but there's a bed in the corner of the other room. Ma will sleep there. I'm taking the loft."

Emily darted her gaze to him and frowned. "Husbands and wives generally share a room."

"That was the original plan, but things changed, remember?"

"I know, but I thought. . ."

"You thought we'd share a room without being intimate?" Jeremiah's face reddened at his bold statement. He stood and walked toward the door. "As I said earlier, a man can only take so much. I'll bring in the rest of your things."

Tears pooled in Emily's eyes as, miserably, she watched him leave and close the door behind him. She stood and began hanging her things in the wardrobe. Jeremiah made two more trips from the wagon, but they didn't speak. When he left for the last time, he informed her supper would be ready in about an hour.

When her things were put away, Emily noted the time. There were still forty-five minutes before she was expected for the meal. The thought of facing the awkward silence was more than she could bear, so she stretched out on the soft mattress. She stared at the ceiling, wishing for all she was worth that events had unfolded differently today.

If only she hadn't listened to Amelia Bell!

thirteen

When Emily didn't emerge for supper, Jeremiah tapped on her door and waited. After a minute he turned the knob and stepped inside. At the sight of his new bride sleeping peacefully on the bed he'd prepared for them to share, Jeremiah's heart stirred within his chest.

He swallowed hard and tiptoed closer, daring a look at her lovely, pale face. Tenderness washed over him. Tears clung to her lashes as though she'd cried herself to sleep. He understood her tears. He wanted Emily to be happy—he'd wanted to bring her here and begin a life together.

Why did you have to put a contract between us, you silly woman? All you have to do is tear it up. . .prove you believe in me, or this is the first of many lonely nights for us both.

She sighed and snuggled deeper into the fluffy mattress. Jeremiah backed slowly away and gently closed the door behind him.

"Well?" Ma asked, setting a pot of stew on the table. "Is she coming or not?"

"She's sleeping, and I hated to wake her. We'll keep her supper warm in case she's hungry later."

Jeremiah grabbed Emily's bowl, grateful that Ma had at least had the courtesy to set a place for his wife. He dipped out a portion of stew and set it on the back of the stove to keep warm. Then he took his place at the table. Ma snorted. "I can see things are going to be different around here from now on."

"Did you have any doubt of that?"

"No, but I didn't expect her to start running things the moment she arrived."

A grin tipped Jeremiah's lips at her exaggeration. "She's

118

sleeping, Ma; how does that translate to her running things?"

Ma's mouth tightened into a firm line. She clasped her hands in front of her and closed her eyes.

Taking the silent hint, Jeremiah bowed his head and said the blessing. When he looked up, Ma's faded gray eyes were narrowed and pensively staring at him.

"I just hope you don't live to regret your hasty marriage like I did."

With a scowl, Jeremiah dipped a generous portion of venison stew into his bowl. "I don't see any comparison."

"Marriages can be hard for many different reasons. Your pa was a bully and a gambler, but at least we knew what to expect from him." She forked a chunk of meat from her bowl and held it suspended in front of her mouth. "I know you. You've loved this girl since you were ten years old. Suddenly you have an opportunity to marry her, and you jump on it like a cat on a mouse. All of your hopes of a family life are wrapped up in this marriage. I just don't want to see you hurt." She took her bite.

Jeremiah sent her a smile. "I know you only care about my happiness, and I appreciate it. But first off, my hopes are firmly set in Christ and my relationship with Him—not my relationship with Emily or anyone else. You taught me long ago that God is faithful even during times of disappointment and struggle. Secondly, I didn't jump on the chance to marry her. I just did the right thing by her—not that I was complaining at the turn of events. And thirdly. . ." He grinned across the table. "I liked her a whole lot when we were ten, but I didn't actually fall in love with her until we were eleven. She pitched the baseball and hit me in the eye. I've been smitten ever since."

Ma chuckled. "I've never seen a person so proud of a shiner in all my born days." Her amusement quickly drained from her lined face, and her eyes grew solemn once more. "But, Son, you're not eleven anymore. The kind of wounds a person can inflict on the one who loves him are a lot more painful than a black eye—believe me, I know all about heartache and black eyes. The bruises were easier to bear."

Jeremiah swallowed his bite of food with difficulty as the old, familiar anger began to burn inside of him. The memory of Ma's bruises, the unreasonable accusations, and the gambling debts clouded his mind, pushing aside dreams of his own marriage.

As though reading his dark thoughts, Ma tapped on the table to gain his attention. "I didn't bring that up to remind you of the bad times, Jeremiah. But I want you to be realistic. Don't set your sights for happiness on Emily. All those dreams you've lived with about her all these years are bound to be a sight prettier than what's to come."

"Don't be such a worrier, Ma. Emily and I will get along just fine."

Ma snorted. "Is that why you moved your things into the loft? I've half a mind to get my Bible out and show that girl a thing or two about a wife's place."

Jeremiah's ears burned. "Ma. . . ," he groaned.

"Oh, hogwash. You're a man now. And I live under this roof too. Did you think I wasn't going to notice?"

"At the very least, I hoped you wouldn't mention it. It's rather indelicate."

"Well, some things just aren't right. That's all. It isn't right for a married man to sleep alone in the loft while his spoiled wife sleeps away the day in the feather bed he labored to restuff for them to share! I'd say that's more than indelicate. It's downright indecent."

She was going to cry! He could hear the catch in her throat. "Ma, would it make you feel better if I toss my wife's things into the loft and sleep in the feather bed myself?"

As predicted, she chortled, keeping the tears at bay. "If I had my way, that's exactly what you'd do, you silly boy." A deep sigh engulfed her, and she gazed upon him with the glow of mother-love. That comforting, familiar look he'd always seen shine from her eyes. "You've been such a good son. How many boys would work at Tucker's and stay in school, then come home and do farm chores like a man? You took care of me after your pa died, when I should have been taking care of you. I was determined to see that you found a good wife who would make you happy, and look—I failed again."

Jeremiah shifted his gaze to his plate. While he appreciated his ma's confidence in him, he knew she saw him through the eyes of an adoring mother. She tended to forget the fact that he had stolen from Tuck over and over before giving his life to the Lord. And since he was the only comfort she had, Jeremiah didn't remind her. But it still made him uncomfortable to be admired so undeservingly.

"I will be happy. You'll see. Once we get used to one another, I'm sure things will just naturally take care of themselves. Remember, I may have loved her all these years, but that doesn't mean she's loved me. As a matter of fact, other than once when we were sixteen, Emily never even noticed me until she bought Tucker's."

He reached across the table and grabbed a warm dinner roll from the basket.

"Well, she should have noticed you!" The change in Ma's tone arrested his attention. He jerked up to meet her flashing eyes. "I would have done anything to have married such a good man, and just look. . .your wife doesn't even share your first supper together with you. Instead, she sleeps right through it and expects you to keep it warm for her!"

"She doesn't expect anything! She just went to sleep. That's all. You can't hold it against her when you wouldn't let her help you cook."

"Are you taking her side against mine? Is this the way it's going to be from now on? Why, I might as well move off somewhere and live alone. I can ask Miss Hastings tomorrow if she has any rooms available at her boardinghouse. I suppose I can take in sewing and washing again to support myself.

I wouldn't want to be a burden on you and your new wife."

Feeling like a brute for making his mother cry, Jeremiah went to her and crouched down next to her chair, gathering her into his arms. "Come now, Ma. You know you're not a burden."

"Are you sure?" She sniffed and accepted his handkerchief. "Perhaps your wife wouldn't mind sharing your bed if I wasn't here. After all, even if she is an old maid, every new bride needs her privacy."

Jeremiah heard a gasp coming from the direction of the bedroom.

With a groan, he glanced up to find Emily staring ashen-faced in the doorway.

❧

She would not give that horrible woman the satisfaction of seeing her cry! Plus, she had half a mind to let her dear mother-in-law know just who decided not to share a bed with whom. Satisfying as blurting it out might be, Emily couldn't imagine actually doing so and ever being able to face Jeremiah again. She simply jerked her chin up and walked to the table where Jeremiah stood holding her chair for her. "I'm sorry. I guess I didn't sleep well last night what with all the excitement of the wedding."

Jeremiah pushed in her chair, then walked to the stove and brought her a bowl filled with stew.

Emily's cheeks warmed. "I could have gotten it myself."

"As any wife should," Mrs. Daniels huffed.

"Ma..."

"Well, I have a right to my say-so, don't I? Wouldn't you say so, Emily dear?" Her smile was a little too sweet after the conversation Emily had just overheard.

"I–I suppose so."

"You see?" She glanced at Jeremiah. "Your wife is an advocate for the rights of women. So don't try to shush me again."

"Rights are one thing," he shot back. "Bad manners are another."

Emily gasped at his disrespectful tone. "It's fine, Jeremiah. Your ma is right. I should have gotten my own supper, and I would have if I had realized you kept it warm on the stove for me. That was. . .very thoughtful of you, Mother Daniels."

"It wasn't my idea," she replied with an ungracious sniff. "I wanted to wake you up."

The woman was obviously spoiling for a fight, and Emily almost obliged. Only Jeremiah's pleading eyes halted her retort.

She took a bite, determined to pay her mother-in-law a compliment whether she deserved one or not. She chewed with relish and relief that she could praise the cook without deception.

"This is delicious, Mother Daniels," she said. "I'd love the recipe."

"Thank you," she replied curtly. "I'm surprised someone like you would be interested in a recipe."

"Someone like me?" Emily narrowed her eyes and captured the woman's challenging gaze. "What do you mean by that?"

"Isn't it rather obvious? A woman who chooses to work rather than taking care of her husband and home surely has no intention of cooking."

"Independence and domesticity aren't mutually exclusive, Ma'am. I have every intention of being a wife to Jeremiah."

Her brow shot up and her lips twisted into a sardonic smile. "Oh, really? Is that why—"

"Ma. Don't. . ."

"Never mind, Jeremiah." Emily's nostrils flared, and her grip tightened on her fork. "Remember, I am all for civil liberties. Your mother has a right to state whatever's on her mind."

Jeremiah's fork clanked against his bowl and he stood suddenly. He swept them both with his disgusted gaze. "I don't have the stomach to listen to your bickering. I'm going out to do the chores. Kindly have this over with before I get back." So saying, he stomped to the door, grabbed his hat from its peg, and left.

"Now see what you've done, young lady? He can't even finish his meal."

"What I've done?" Emily closed her eyes, fighting for control. "I think we've gotten off on the wrong foot. I'm sorry for sounding testy. Since we're going to be living under the same roof, I think we had better try to get along—for all of our sakes, but particularly Jeremiah's."

A glint of grudging respect appeared in the woman's eyes, and Emily felt the hope rising. "I'll clean up the supper dishes," she offered.

"No need for that. I've been cleaning my own kitchen for forty years. I will continue doing so. You have your store to attend and Jeremiah has his. I'll attend to the house and cooking."

"But. . ." Emily didn't know what to say. She wanted to do the things wives were supposed to do. Cook, clean, wash her husband's shirts. Share his bed. Give him sons and daughters. But that wasn't the life Jeremiah had offered her. He had offered her a home. Period. A lonely bed in which to sleep at night. And a mother-in-law who clearly despised her.

Fine. Let Mother Daniels make her meals and wash her dishes. Emily was determined to find a way to make Jeremiah see that she could still be a wife to him whether she retained her contract between them or not. She had to make him see that every woman had the right—no, the responsibility—to protect her interests. And she had to do so without Jeremiah finding out that she'd overheard his humiliating conversation with Harold Baxter.

Who knew? She might even win her mother-in-law over to the suffragette movement. The woman certainly had the spirit for it.

Emily's lips curved upward at the thought.

fourteen

The wagon swayed with the ruts. Emily pressed against Jeremiah; and even though he knew it wasn't intentional, he couldn't help but enjoy the sensation of her arm against his. She righted herself immediately and resumed her ramrod straight position on the wagon seat. Ma sat on Emily's other side. . .equally silent, equally straight.

Three weeks. . .he'd been a groom for three weeks, and the women in his life were driving him crazy. They didn't bicker anymore. Thankfully. Now they were polite. And at times that was worse than the arguing.

He should have refused to drive them to town tonight and would have, except he wasn't sure they'd both make it home in one piece if he left them to their own devices.

It seemed ridiculous to him that he'd be dropping them off at the town hall so that Emily could give a speech inside while his ma protested from without. Downright embarrassing.

Give me the patience of Job, Lord. Because unless these two women You've placed in my life come to a meeting of minds soon— one way or another—I'm afraid I'll have to move out to the barn.

The wagon rolled onto the street, and slowly they made their way toward the hall. Jeremiah groaned. It seemed more folks had turned out tonight than had shown up to the Christmas pageant. He figured they were curious, knowing his mother— president of the League of Christian Women—would be the first in line to protest the unwomanly behavior of the suffragettes whom his wife supported.

A tug on his sleeve pulled him from his thoughts. He stared dumbly at Emily.

"Where are you going, Jeremiah?"

"You rolled right past the hall. Everyone is staring."

Heat crept up his neck. "Sorry. My mind was in the clouds."

Emily gave him a shy smile. "No harm done."

Jeremiah's heart raced at the upward curve of her full lips. He patted her hand, which still clutched his sleeve. She released it immediately and ducked her head. Inwardly, he smiled. Perhaps it wouldn't be long. She cared for him. He knew she did. Soon she'd realize she could trust him. And when she did, she would tear up that contract and come to him, knowing he'd never try to make her do something against her will. He wasn't anything like his pa.

"Just let us out here," she said. "We can walk a few steps back to the hall while you go on and find a place to tether the team."

"That all right with you, Ma?"

"We're already a spectacle," Ma huffed. "Might as well be a bigger one—imagine, the two of us walking together."

"How about if I let Emily off here, and then I can circle the team around and drop you off in front of the hall?"

"Don't be ridiculous. Everyone already saw us ride in together. We'd look even more foolish if you did that. We'll just get down here."

Jeremiah hopped from the wagon and extended his arms to Emily. She slid over without catching his gaze and allowed him to lift her down. So intent was he on the pleasant feel of his wife in his arms, Jeremiah failed to notice a deep crevice in the ground. Just as he turned her loose, she gasped and grappled for him, trying to keep from losing her footing in the wagon wheel rut.

In a flash, Jeremiah reached out and grabbed hold of her waist to steady her. It was a natural reaction, he told himself, to pull her closer—instinctive, really.

"Thank you," she whispered, withdrawing slightly, but not actually pulling away.

Jeremiah's heart soared at the way she molded perfectly

against him. The top of her head reached just under his chin, so that if she raised her head a bit and he bent ever so slightly. . . So help him, he'd give a front tooth for the courage to kiss her soundly right here and now. He gathered a deep breath, seriously contemplating the temptation, when Ma's loud clearing of the throat brought him back to reality.

"The two of you stop it immediately," Ma hissed.

With a gasp, Emily stepped back. Jeremiah resented the cold, empty void replacing her warmth. When he was sure she had her footing, he walked around and helped Ma from the wagon.

She gave him a cold, silent glare, raised her chin, and fell into step beside Emily.

Jeremiah watched them, each holding her head erect, shoulders straight, and striding purposefully toward the hall. With a sigh, he climbed back into the wagon and flapped the reins. He resumed his earlier, silent prayer.

Yes, Lord. I need the patience of Job to get through these trials. Either that or a nice warm bed in the barn ought to do it.

ஐ

Emily cast a sideways glance at her mother-in-law and sighed. The Lord knew she'd been trying to get along with Mother Daniels; but, honestly, the woman sure didn't make it easy. Honey dripped from her lips when she spoke to her son and turned to vinegar before any words directed at Emily reached her ears.

The Bible said sweet and bitter waters couldn't flow from the same cistern, but Emily had proof that this woman definitely had an inward switch to make that possible. She smiled to herself. No, the Word wasn't wrong; but she couldn't quite figure out how to let those sweet words flow in her direction.

It wasn't as though she wasn't trying. No matter how hard she tried, she couldn't do anything to please the woman.

Tensions had been running high the last couple of days as each prepared for tonight. But Emily didn't want to make an enemy because of her beliefs. She only wanted to have the right to express them and not be ridiculed or despised because of that expression. Didn't they both love God? Weren't they both Christians? Why couldn't they live together without ungodly strife?

She felt she needed to speak candidly, or the woman would be impossible to live with in the upcoming days.

Halting, she reached for Mrs. Daniels. "Wait just a moment, please."

"What is it? Everyone is waiting for me."

"Yes, Ma'am. I'll hurry, I promise. But there's something I want to say. I'm not sure how. . .but I want you to know, I don't want us to be enemies. We're family now, and I'd very much like it if we can be friends."

"Why are you bringing this up now, of all times?" Mrs. Daniels scowled. "You have a knack for doing things at the inappropriate time, Girl. And I don't mind saying so."

"I don't know what you mean." Emily's stomach tightened at the disappointment of having her efforts thrown back into her face.

"You and Jeremiah." Disgust thickened her tone.

"Did I do something inappropriate with Jeremiah?" Her face warmed, knowing exactly what Mrs. Daniels was getting at, but hoping she'd let it pass in the spirit of propriety.

However, as Emily had come to understand all too well, Jeremiah's mother chose carefully the topics she considered proper; and apparently, she didn't have a qualm about this particular topic.

"It's ridiculous. You won't kiss my son at home, and yet right there on the street you use the oldest trick around to try and get one from him." She shook her head. "Believe me, you don't have to resort to trickery to get a kiss from a man. Especially one who's as smitten as my son is."

Emily felt the outrage from the tips of her toes to the top of her head. "What trick?" she asked, her voice suddenly shrill.

"Oh, come now. Tripping when you get out of the wagon so he has to catch you before you fall?"

"That was an accident!"

"So you say. From where I sat, it looked mighty fishy."

"Then perhaps you need to purchase a pair of spectacles," Emily retorted.

"Well!" Mrs. Daniels pivoted and stomped away.

"Wait!"

The older woman spun around, her lips twisted downward, brow furrowed.

"Wh—what do you mean he's smitten?"

"Oh, for mercy's sake. What do you think I mean?"

Emily let her go this time, her heart about to explode with the joy of the merest hint that Jeremiah was smitten with her. He had told Amelia Bell he was sweet on her and that he wouldn't mind her printing it in the newspaper, but Emily had assumed he was just trying to get under her skin. Now she wasn't so sure.

On the other hand, perhaps Mrs. Daniels was wrong. She hadn't been the one to overhear Jeremiah talking with Harold about running her store. And the woman had certainly been wrong about her recent accusation. Emily fumed. Imagine the audacity! Accusing her of trying to finagle a kiss.

A guilty little shiver rubbed down her spine. Maybe she had taken advantage of the situation. But she certainly didn't cause it. And there wasn't a thing wrong with a woman offering her husband a kiss of thanks for saving her from a tumble in the street.

"Where do you think you're going, Woman?"

Emily gasped and stopped short at the gruff voice, then realized the words came from the opposite side of the street and weren't directed at her. She peered closer, her heart beating rapidly as she spied Mr. and Mrs. Gregory.

"Did you hear me? I asked where you think you're going." He had her by the shoulders and shook her hard until her hair came free from its pins and fell down her back.

"Please, don't make a scene," the woman pleaded. "Let's just go home."

"Now you want to go home? I told you, you're not to go near that meeting hall tonight, didn't I?"

"I—I'm sorry."

"You're sorry you got caught. Thought I wouldn't be home tonight. Thought I didn't know you sneak off to those meetings when I'm not around."

Unable to look away, Emily watched the exchange, her stomach quivering. She had seen Mrs. Gregory at the meetings and wondered how she'd managed to convince her husband to allow it. Now she realized the truth. Tears stung her eyes, and she debated whether to run across the street and rescue the poor woman. But she knew it would do no good. *Please watch over Mrs. Gregory, dear Lord.*

With a heavy heart, she turned back toward the hall.

"Do you see what your ideas have created, Mrs. Daniels?"

Dread engulfed Emily as she realized that, this time, Mr. Gregory was calling to her.

Facing the street, she swallowed hard. "My ideas are creating good things, Sir. Hopefully, before long, the law will favor a woman and not allow her husband to bully her. Now if you'll excuse me, I have a speech to give. Good day, Mrs. Gregory. I'll pray for you."

Knees wobbly, she mustered her courage and stomped away.

She halted close to the hall, hating the thought of shouldering her way through the crowd of protesting women blocking the steps. She wasn't afraid of bodily harm, for she knew none of them would accost her in that manner. But she detested the disapproving whispers, the stares, the implications about her womanhood. Still, better that than Mr. Gregory's brand of disapproval.

"Come on, I'll walk you in."

Emily turned at the sound of Jeremiah's voice next to her.

"That was fast."

"I found a close spot. I've been following you." He took her chilled hand, warming her as he laced his fingers through hers. "That was some speech you gave already."

"You witnessed my exchange with Mr. Gregory?"

He nodded grimly. "I thought I might have to take care of him."

Emily's heart turned over at the iron in his tone. "I'm glad you didn't." She gave him a teasing grin. "After all, didn't you say you're not much of a fighter? Besides, if I can take on your ma, I can handle a bully like Mr. Gregory."

"Something happen between you and Ma?"

"We had words," she admitted.

He groaned. "What did you argue about? Never mind, don't tell me. It's better if I don't know."

She grinned. "I wasn't going to tell you, anyway. Your mother and I made a pact that we wouldn't involve you in our disagreements."

"That explains the unbearable silence at suppertime."

Emily couldn't keep back her smile. "We could stop holding back on your account."

He gazed warmly at her and grinned in return, nearly snatching Emily's breath away. "I think I'd prefer to suffer the silence."

He seemed unaware of the havoc his nearness was wreaking on her—legs trembled, cheeks were warm, and she was quite possibly heading for a dead faint—although she couldn't be sure since she'd never actually fainted before.

Squeezing her fingers, he leaned in close and whispered against her ear, "Time to face the gauntlet. Don't worry, I'll protect you."

His teasing tone eased her tension, and she elbowed him playfully. "The main one you have to protect me from is your ma."

To Emily's relief, the sight of Jeremiah firmly stationed at her side seemed to drain a bit of spunk from the ladies. The crowd moved back, creating a path for them to the door.

"Just where do you think you're going?" Mother Daniels took one step and blocked the entrance. She ignored Emily, focusing her gaze upon Jeremiah.

He leaned forward and kissed his mother's cheek, then whispered something into her ear. Concern shot through Emily as the woman's face drained of color, and sudden tears pooled in her eyes before she ducked her head, stepping aside.

Jeremiah ushered Emily inside.

"What on earth did you say to her? You made your mother cry."

"I did?" He looked genuinely surprised. "You must be mistaken."

"I most certainly am not mistaken. I know tears when I see them!"

A scowl marred his features. "You two are driving me to distraction! All I said was that my wife is giving a speech tonight, and I intend to be in here to support you."

"Oh." Emily wanted to say so much more. Just as she opened her mouth, Amelia grabbed her.

"Nice to see you here, Jeremiah." She beamed at him. "I have to borrow Emily, but you can have her back right after the rally."

"I'm counting on it." He kept his gaze focused squarely on Emily. She wished Amelia would go away. As a matter of fact, she wished everyone would go away. She could do without the noisy women gearing up for the rally and the chanters outside expressing their displeasure with those women— including her. They could all just go away!

Who cared about her dumb speech anyway? What did any of it matter?

At this moment, she only cared about one right—the right to be alone with her husband.

fifteen

Jeremiah grinned as he helped Emily into the wagon and climbed up beside her to wait for Ma.

"You gave a good speech tonight. Even better than the first one."

The warmth of Emily's smile cut through the chilly, late February night and wrapped around him like a pair of arms.

She sent him a saucy look from her cat-green eyes—a flirtatious look, pleasing Jeremiah a great deal. "You're a hero," she said. "I believe every woman in town envies me. I may have to keep an eye on the unmarried girls."

"Jealous?"

She shook her head, her eyes sparkling in the lantern light. "Proud."

Jeremiah chuckled. "Isn't that a sin?"

"Maybe. Although I'm not sure that kind of pride is the same kind that God hates. But just to be on the safe side. . . How about, I'm feeling incredibly blessed and thankful for your support?"

She reached over and pressed her palm against his arm. "Thank you, Jeremiah."

He'd felt incredibly blessed himself as he watched his wife stand before all those women and be admired. Emily had displayed a new confidence as she proudly stated that he supported her efforts to run her own business.

He took her hand and brought it to his lips, capturing her gaze.

She stared back at him, and he recognized the look of love shining in her eyes.

Leaning close, he rested his head against the top of hers.

"I'd kiss you if we weren't in the middle of town," he whispered, pressing their clasped hands close to his heart.

"I'd kiss you back." Hearing the smile in her voice, Jeremiah inhaled deeply, taking in the scent of lilacs wafting from her hair.

She released a soft sigh, and Jeremiah's heart beat a rapid rhythm against his chest. Where was Ma anyway? The quicker she showed up, the quicker they could get home, away from the town's prying eyes. Because he had every intention of claiming that kiss.

Sobering at the thought of what Ma would have to say to him about entering that building tonight, he came crashing back to earth. He might be practically a hero with the suffragettes, but he was far from a hero with the ladies in town who represented the other view. To their way of thinking, he was a traitor, a bad son, and most likely bullied by his aggressive, independent wife. Why couldn't folks tend to their own business and leave him alone?

"What's wrong?" Emily's brow furrowed. "Thinking about your ma?" Her voice rang with sympathy.

"Partly. And partly I was thinking about other folks and their wrong ideas about you and some of the other women who were there tonight."

"Like my brothers thinking Mr. Krenshaw is a sissy because his wife is in the movement?"

Nodding, Jeremiah straightened in the wagon seat, but still kept her hand grasped in his.

"But you see how Mrs. and Mr. Krenshaw are together. She adores her husband and he adores her. He is just a very forward-thinking man. I don't see why folks have to make issues out of things that are none of their affair."

"Well, she does smoke cigars and wear men's britches," Jeremiah drawled.

"True. . ." Emily nibbled her bottom lip. "But that doesn't mean she bullies her husband, does it?"

"No."

"And they never show up to services on Sundays, so I don't believe they know Jesus. That doesn't mean she wears the pants in the family. . .well, you know what I mean."

"I do. And no, I don't think she wears the figurative pants in the family. But I am afraid most folks think so, and there's nothing we can do to change their minds."

Emily sat up straighter in the seat and squared her shoulders. "I intend to do everything I can to change folks' minds. It's just not right for a man to be spoken poorly of because his wife wants to vote. Land sakes, they let us vote for school board positions, why not state and federal officials? It's nonsense."

"I agree."

She regarded him with a raised brow. "You really do? You're not just pretending to save face?"

"Is that what you thought tonight?"

"I considered it. After all, how many of the men inside, other than Mr. Krenshaw, of course, honestly support their wives, and how many are just showing up so they get their suppers cooked and their beds warmed?"

"You probably have a point, but there is always the chance that the men appreciate the value of a good strong opinion coming from someone with a lot of sense." Jeremiah squeezed her hand. "I think this country would do well to allow women like you to vote. As a matter of fact, there are quite a few men whose votes might cause more harm than good."

Emily's laughter rang loudly into the air. She threw her arms about his neck, nearly knocking him backward from the wagon in her exuberance.

"Well, I can see you weren't too worried about my absence." Ma's cold voice pulled them apart. She stood next to Miss Hastings. "Myra has graciously informed me she has a vacancy."

"Ma, what are you talking about? You don't need to move into the boardinghouse."

"I wouldn't stay another night in that house, knowing that I'm not wanted. It's obvious that wife of yours has poisoned your mind with all this women's rights nonsense—enough so that you would betray your own mother—publicly humiliate me!"

"Mother Daniels, please. Jeremiah didn't—"

"I am not speaking to you, young lady, and don't call me 'Mother Daniels.' And don't pretend you aren't happy to be rid of me."

"But I don't want you to move out of your home on my account." Emily's voice trembled. She tried to pull her hand away, but Jeremiah kept it firmly grasped in his.

"Ma, how about coming home and we'll discuss all of this in private?"

She raised her chin stubbornly. "There's nothing to discuss. I will get the wagon from the livery while you two are at your stores tomorrow and will pack my things. And don't worry, I intend to hire Billy Simpson to help me, so you won't be bothered."

"You're never any bother, Ma."

Hurt clouded her eyes. "So you're willing to help me move out? I knew you wanted to be rid of me."

Jeremiah released Emily's hand and climbed down. "Ma, Emily and I want you to stay at home where you belong. Give up this silly idea and let me help you into the wagon."

Ma lifted her chin stubbornly. "My mind's made up. Come, Myra, let's get home."

"At least let me drive you and Miss Hastings over to the boardinghouse."

"No, thank you, we'd prefer to walk."

"Then let me walk with you. There are still some icy patches on the sidewalk."

"Then we'll walk on the road."

"Be careful on the road too. There are deep ruts. Remember Emily stumbled earlier."

"That is a matter of debate."

From the wagon seat, Jeremiah heard Emily gasp.

"Ma, wait. I'm coming with you."

"I am not a child," she snapped. "I can certainly walk a few feet without your help."

"Yes, Ma'am," Jeremiah said with a sigh.

He watched her walk away, then climbed into the wagon.

"I'm so sorry, Jeremiah," Emily said, self-condemnation evident in her tone. "Regardless of our differences, I never wanted your ma to move out."

"This isn't your fault, Honey. Ma's got a stubborn streak a mile wide, and I stepped on it tonight when I walked into that hall."

"I wouldn't have been mad at you if you had chosen to stay away," Emily said quietly.

He reached forward and tipped her chin until she met his gaze. "I went because I believe in you, not to keep you from becoming angry with me. And I want everyone to know I believe in you."

Her expression softened, and her eyes looked almost liquid in the moonlight. Drawing a swift breath, he lowered his head. Just as he claimed her eager lips, a scream filled the air.

Heart in his throat, Jeremiah grabbed the reins and drove the short distance to the source of the scream. Seeing his mother crumpled in the street, he felt his heart in his throat. He halted the horses and gave the reins to Emily, then sprinted to his mother's side and fell to his knees.

"What happened?" he asked Miss Hastings.

The woman trembled, and her voice shook. "As you said might happen, she twisted her ankle in one of the wagon tracks. She fell before I could reach out to steady her."

"Ma, I'm going to have to lift you in order to put you in the back of the wagon. We'll take you home while someone rides for Doc St. John, okay?"

Ma nodded and attempted a slight smile, but it fell short

and instead appeared as a grimace.

Emily pressed gently on Jeremiah's arm. "I'm going to grab some blankets from my store so she doesn't have to lie down on the wood."

Without waiting for an answer, Emily flew the few feet to Emily's Place and made it back to the street in record time. She quickly spread several blankets in the back of the wagon.

Ma moaned softly when Jeremiah lifted her from the ground. She fainted by the time she was settled into the bed of the wagon. He released a relieved sigh that she was free from pain for a little while. Her leg had felt twisted in his arms, and he knew it was badly broken.

He drove as quickly as he could without jostling her too much. Emily remained quiet next to him. He wanted to comfort her. . .to reassure her that this wasn't her fault, but he was struggling with his own guilt on the matter. Why hadn't he just insisted Ma come home? All she had wanted was some reassurance that he still needed her and wanted her around. The truth of the matter was, he'd been so focused on getting alone with his wife that he hadn't tried nearly hard enough to dissuade Ma from staying the night at Miss Hastings's.

They finally arrived at the farm and settled Ma into Emily's bed. He knew when Ma came to, she'd protest sleeping there, but Emily had insisted.

Emily's brother, Sam, the town physician, arrived within minutes. Emily ushered him into the bedroom, and she and Jeremiah paced the sitting room until he emerged a few minutes later.

"How bad is she?" Jeremiah asked. "I reckon she broke her leg?"

Sam nodded solemnly. "I'm afraid so. I need to set it quickly, and of course she'll have to stay in bed until it heals."

"Of course."

"How long until she heals up, Sam?" Emily asked, her eyes soft with sympathy.

"I'm not sure. Quite some time, maybe. She may never regain full use of that leg. As a matter of fact, I'd say it's doubtful she'll ever walk unaided by a walking stick at least."

He glanced at Jeremiah. "I could use some help setting the leg and getting it in a splint. You up to it?"

Jeremiah's stomach churned, but he nodded. He followed Sam into the bedroom and held Ma still while Sam set the bones. After the splint was on and the leg tightly wrapped, Sam regarded Jeremiah soberly. "She's going to need one hundred percent care for awhile. Your ma can't even attempt to use that leg for several weeks. If she tries, she may break it worse and lose all hope of ever walking again. Make sure she knows that."

"I will."

Sam snapped his bag shut and headed for the sitting room. He bent and kissed Emily on the cheek.

"How is she, Sam?" Emily asked, her eyes clouded with worry.

"Still sleeping. I used a little chloroform to make sure she didn't wake up while I was working on her leg, so she'll probably sleep through the night. I left a bottle of laudanum for when the pain is too much for her to bear. But use it sparingly so she doesn't come to rely on it."

Listening to Emily question her brother, Jeremiah couldn't help but think if Ma could only see how much Emily cared about her, perhaps the barbs and insinuations would stop. Perhaps she could meet his wife somewhere in the middle.

Sam clapped his hat on his head and headed for the door.

"Sam—wait. How do we care for her?"

"Jeremiah will fill you in. Just be careful around her leg, and don't let her get up."

With a frustrated sigh, she closed the door after him and turned to Jeremiah. "I wish he could have told us more."

Jeremiah repeated Sam's counsel and instructions. "I'll ask around and perhaps hire a girl to cook and clean and care for Ma."

Emily's face drained of color and her lips trembled. "You don't think I can do all that?"

"You have the store to run. I was only thinking of hiring someone to do the things Ma usually does around here and to tend to her while we're gone."

"Jeremiah, if you don't mind, I'd rather hire someone to look after the store for me so I can stay and take care of your mother."

His jaw dropped open. Never in a million years had he considered Emily for the job. "Do you think that's a good idea?"

Emily shrugged. "I think it's a God idea. It came to me as I was praying. Work can't come before family. A woman has needs that her son simply can't attend to, so you can't stay home with her. But she needs family, not hired help."

"She'll eat you alive, Honey. Are you sure God gave you this idea?"

"Who else?"

Jeremiah didn't want to say who sprang to mind.

Emily scowled. "It wasn't the devil. I know it doesn't look like a good idea. But sometimes the worst ones turn out to be the best. Who knows, maybe your ma will learn to love me like a daughter."

Lacking the heart to further discourage her, Jeremiah smiled warmly. "Maybe you're right."

Emily smiled brightly. "Thank you, Jeremiah. I know this is for the best."

sixteen

"Emileeeeee!"

"Just a minute," Emily growled under her breath. She slammed Jeremiah's wet shirt against the washboard and straightened up, stretching her aching back. She sighed. Her every effort over the past few weeks had been met with scorn, and Mother Daniels's constant need for attention nearly drove Emily to distraction. She had truly hoped their time together would improve the woman's opinion of her, but if anything, it had worsened.

Feeling guilty for her sour thoughts, Emily determined to be extra pleasant this trip inside. She dried her hands on her apron and refrained from stomping into the house. "Yes, Mother Daniels?" she asked, entering the bedroom.

"I need another pillow at my back. I'd like to read for awhile."

Emily couldn't fault her for wanting a little entertainment. After weeks in bed, anyone would be touchy. But with all of these interruptions, how was a body to get anything done?

She grabbed a pillow and gently adjusted it under the older woman's shoulders. "How's that?"

"A little high."

Irritation niggled Emily's stomach. She adjusted the pillow again. "This?"

"Yes, it's fine now."

"All right, then," Emily said, forcing a cheery smile. "I'll get back to my washing."

A grimace crossed Mother Daniels's face.

"Are you in pain?"

"No. You run along. I don't want to keep you." The grimace again.

Emily hesitated. "Then what is it?"

"What is what?"

"You looked like you wanted to say something." And it didn't look like a pleasant something, she wanted to add, but didn't.

"It's nothing. You have better things to do than take care of an old woman."

Biting back a retort and resisting the temptation to roll her eyes, Emily dug deep inside and tried to find compassion for her mother-in-law. After all, she couldn't imagine having to stay cooped up day in and day out with only four walls staring back at her. "Nonsense," she assured her mother-in-law. "What can I do for you?"

Her mouth tightened into something resembling a grudging smile. "Well, since you insist, I could do with a nice mug of coffee." She gave Emily a sharp glance. "Only, be careful not to get it too strong this time. This morning's coffee nearly choked me."

And yet it hadn't stopped her from asking for a second cup. Emily refused to begin a war of words with the ungrateful matron. Rather, she smiled. "All right, I'll do my best to make it a little more to your liking."

"Thank you. If you're sure it's not too much trouble."

"No trouble at all." *Unless you happen to have piles of laundry to do.*

Emily made her way into the front room and grabbed the coffee beans from the shelf above the stove. She ground the beans, then took the coffeepot to the outside pump to fill it with water. On her way back to the house, she eyed her pile of half-washed laundry and grimaced. At this rate, she'd never have it all finished before Jeremiah returned from town. And she so wanted to prove herself useful in household duties.

While the coffee boiled, she decided to start their supper. Jeremiah had shot and killed two rabbits the day before and had mentioned a "hankering" for some slow-roasted rabbit. Emily had been planning tonight's meal ever since.

She went to the root cellar, grabbed the rabbits and some preserved vegetables, then headed back to the kitchen.

Twenty minutes later, she gave a happy nod and resumed scrubbing clothes. Mother Daniels was occupied with a recent dime novel and her cup of coffee, slightly sweetened as she liked. To Emily's delight, the woman had actually smiled her thanks and expressed her satisfaction with the taste of the coffee.

The house filled with the smell of cooking meat and onions, and Emily's stomach rumbled, reminding her that she hadn't eaten since breakfast; but she decided against stopping for food. She had precious little time to finish her chores without taking time to eat.

A smile touched her lips as her stomach grumbled again. Another blessing that had come from weeks of hard work at home was that her clothes were getting loose on her. And she'd learned to push away her plate after one helping. Though she was far from having the trim figure she'd always craved, she would at least have to take in most of her dresses at the waist before long.

She worked throughout the afternoon, scrubbing the clothing, boiling them, then rinsing. By the time she had hung the last piece of laundry to dry, her hands were red and raw from the soap, wrinkled from the water, and aching from scrubbing and wringing. Still, a sense of satisfaction came over her as she put away the washtub, boiling pot, and scrub board.

Walking into the house, she had to laugh at herself. Over the months of working at the store, she'd become soft to the hard life of a prairie woman. Even before she bought Tucker's, there had been enough women living at the ranch to share the load. Doing it alone was much more of a challenge than she'd ever thought it would be.

She perked her ear to listen for Mother Daniels and breathed a sigh of relief at the silence. The last time Emily had checked on her, the older woman had been sleeping with her book face down across her chest. She must still be napping.

Emily opened the oven and took in the heavenly aroma wafting out to greet her senses. "Mmmm," she said aloud. Jeremiah would be pleased. She felt her cheeks warm at the thought.

Lately her mind didn't seem to stray far from events occurring the night of her speech—before her mother-in-law's accident. . .the near-kiss beside the wagon, Jeremiah's proud grin during her speech, but most of all, what had happened afterward. Jeremiah's lips had touched hers briefly. She could still feel their softness, the sweetness—the longing. Her stomach lurched at the memory, and a giggle bubbled up inside of her.

She'd loved Jeremiah Daniels since she was ten years old, when he'd molded a turtle out of clay during class one day. She'd spied that turtle on Mother Daniels's knickknack shelf soon after she married Jeremiah. The lesson at school had been about allowing God to mold one's life. Jeremiah had certainly turned his life around that day. The change in him, from that point on, had been noticeable. And soon after that, he'd begun working for Mr. Tucker.

Emily sighed. Jeremiah deserved that store. Why had she been so stubborn? Refusing to share with him just because he hadn't married her for love.

Satisfied that the rabbits were doing well, Emily shut the oven door. How could she keep the store from him when he wanted it so badly? The fact remained that she'd made certain vows before God—that she would love him and be his helpmeet forever. A true helpmeet wouldn't withhold the thing that would make her husband the happiest. Jeremiah wanted Tucker's.

The truth of the matter was that as much as she enjoyed running the store, she also enjoyed caring for the house and Jeremiah. Given a choice, she'd prefer to relinquish the store and stay home. The thought filled her with joy. No matter the reason for their marriage, Emily knew Jeremiah cared for her. How could she doubt it after the tenderness he'd shown her? The desire she saw in his eyes as he watched her go about the house. The long, searching looks he gave her whenever she found the courage to meet his gaze.

She felt her heart race as a collage of memories flooded her. Each brush of his hand against her back or her elbow when he helped her into or out of the wagon filled her with longing, and the warmth of his hand as he held hers during the mealtime blessing made it difficult for her to concentrate on the prayer. She knew he felt the same way.

A plan emerged, and she grinned broadly. Only one thing stood in the way of her and Jeremiah having a true marriage—that contract. And she had every intention of getting rid of the obstacle.

A niggling of worry squirmed inside of her. What of Mother Daniels? She had made it perfectly clear she wouldn't give up taking care of the house. But surely two reasonable women could find an amicable way to share the load, couldn't they? The more she turned it over, the more Emily thought the idea might work.

She practiced a few words in her mind, then tiptoed to the bedroom.

"Mother Daniels?" she whispered, determined to have a heart-to-heart talk before Jeremiah came home. After all, whether she liked Emily or not, the fact remained that she loved her son more than life and would do anything to see him happy. To that end, Emily knew they had to find a way to compromise and work together in regards to the house.

"Yes?" A grouchy, sleepy voice greeted her.

"May I come in? I think we need to talk. . . ."

❧

Sunday morning dawned bright, the weather just right for a late spring morning. Not too warm, not too cold. Jeremiah climbed from the loft, following the wonderful scents of coffee boiling, bacon frying, and biscuits baking in the oven.

He'd been up for hours, finished morning chores, cleaned up, and now looked forward to a nice leisurely breakfast with his wife before attending services in town.

Their marriage wasn't all it could be, but it wasn't entirely unpleasant either. With Ma's injury, Emily had certainly proven herself a capable housekeeper and cook. And over the last couple of weeks, he'd noticed camaraderie between the two women that was nothing short of miraculous. He sent a silent prayer of thanks heavenward. An answered prayer.

He had to admit, though, that he'd missed having Emily ride into town with him over the past few weeks. He missed looking across the street and peeking in on her through the large store window. Her sister, Hope, was doing a competent job of minding the store, but she was no Emily.

Now that Ma was ready to get around with a walking stick, he figured it wouldn't be long before Emily joined him for the daily ride to town once more.

He released a low chuckle as he turned on the bottom rung to find Emily pushing a loose strand of hair from her forehead, leaving a streak of flour in its place.

Her eyebrows shot up. "What's so funny?"

"You." He closed the short distance between them in a couple of strides. "Hold still," he said. Reaching forward, he thumbed away the flour. "There you go."

Splotches of red appeared on Emily's cheeks. "Thank you."

"You're welcome."

"Sit down, and I'll bring your coffee."

Jeremiah sat and watched while she pulled a mug from the shelf above the stove. He frowned.

"What's wrong with your dress?" he asked.

"What do you mean?" She set his cup in front of him, and he caught her around the waist.

"This." He pulled on the material. "You're swimming in this. You feeling poorly?"

"P–poorly? I suppose I've lost a few pounds since I took over the house for your ma. Do I look sick?"

Her eyes flooded with hurt, and her voice sounded strained.

"I guess I didn't notice. You don't look sick. Just different. I'm sorry you're working so hard. Maybe I should hire someone to help you out until Ma's ready to take back over."

"Oh, but. . . Well, if you don't think I'm doing it right."

Jeremiah tenderly searched her face. And suddenly he realized his wife had blossomed over the last couple of months. She exhibited a true joy he'd never observed in her during all the years they'd known each other. Confusion swept over him. That was something he'd have to ponder further to understand. For now, he needed to undo the hurt he'd inadvertently caused her.

On impulse, he scooted his chair away from the table and gently pressed her waist until she had no choice but to pull away from him or take steps toward him. She didn't resist when he pulled her onto his lap.

"What are you doing?" she asked breathlessly.

"Something I've wanted to do for quite some time. Do you mind?"

She smiled and shook her head.

Taking her hand, he brought it to his lips, then nestled it close against his chest.

"In answer to your question, no, you don't look sickly. You're beautiful. You're always beautiful. I just hadn't noticed how thin you've gotten."

Emily laughed. "I'm not thin by any means. As a matter of fact, I could stand to lose more to be like Tarah or Hope. Even Amelia."

"You're perfect." And he meant it. Emily was perfect for him. If only she'd realize how unnecessary that contract between them was. "And the work you do around here is more than acceptable. It's wonderful. I suppose Ma will be taking over again soon," he said, then could have kicked himself as her expression dropped.

"I suppose so." She rose, leaving his arms aching for her to return. He fought the urge to pull her back. "I have to check the bacon before it burns."

"I'll enjoy your company again during our rides to and from town."

She slipped the sizzling bacon onto a platter, then turned to him. "You will?"

"I miss you. I enjoy our talks. Who else in town understands and appreciates talk about running a mercantile?"

"We could talk about it in the evenings, like we do now."

"I know. But I enjoy having you all to myself for a few minutes twice a day. We don't get much time alone at home."

A loud cough caught their attention, and Jeremiah nearly fell from his chair at the sight of Ma standing in the bedroom doorway. He inwardly groaned. Why couldn't he watch his mouth?

"Ma! What are you doing out of bed?"

She leaned heavily on the walking stick he'd whittled for her upon Sam's suggestion. "I think it's about time for me to try this thing out. Besides, I have a hankerin' to join you and your wife for breakfast and then Sunday services."

"Why, that's wonderful!" Emily went to her. "Let me help you to the table."

Embarrassed that he hadn't offered first, Jeremiah stood and strode across the room. He took his mother's free hand. "Here, let me."

"Both of you sit. I can make it alone."

Jeremiah and Emily exchanged glances, and with unspoken agreement, each stayed on one side of her as she moved with painstaking slowness to the table. She was breathing heavily by the time she accepted the chair Jeremiah held out for her.

"Now," she said. "Let's have our breakfast and get to the service. You two have plans for this afternoon."

Jeremiah glanced at her sharply.

Emily drew in a breath. "Today? Are you certain you want to be left alone that long?"

"Quite certain. I'm sure I'll be worn to a frazzle by the time we return from the service and in need of a nice long nap. Plenty of time for what you have planned."

"Does one of you want to inform me of our plans?" Jeremiah asked, exasperated at being left in the dark.

"Nope." Ma's eyes crinkled at the corners. "Your wife has a surprise for you, and I'm not going to be the one to spill the beans."

Jeremiah sent Emily a questioning look, but she merely smiled. "Sit down and have your breakfast, Jeremiah. You'll find out in good time."

Her eyes flashed in saucy determination. Jeremiah grinned and complied. From the way Emily and Ma were smiling at each other, whatever the surprise, it was bound to be a good one.

seventeen

"Thank you. This has been a wonderful surprise," Jeremiah said.

Emily smiled at her husband. They'd enjoyed a nice lunch together, and now he stretched out on the blanket, resting jauntily on his elbow. She walked the short distance to the creek and rinsed off their dishes, keenly aware of Jeremiah's gaze upon her. He'd watched her all day—every single move she made. The attention sent a thrill through Emily, and the hunger in his eyes made her dizzy and nervous at the same time.

The wind whipped at her skirts as she set the picnic basket into the back of the wagon. Nervously, Emily searched the darkening skies. She had planned to produce the contract now and offer Emily's Place to Jeremiah. But she wanted to do so when they wouldn't be interrupted. And from the looks of the clouds, it wouldn't be long before the entire prairie was soaked with rain—including them, if they didn't find shelter soon.

"Jeremiah," she said. "I think we should go home. Look at the sky to the west."

Jeremiah glanced in the direction she pointed and hopped up from the blanket. "You're right," he said, regret thick in his voice. "Much as I hate to cut this day short, we should probably head to the farm."

Emily waited while he snatched up the blanket and pitched it into the back of the wagon. He joined her where she stood waiting for him to offer his assistance. She glanced at him expectantly. He made no move to help her, however. Instead, he reached forward and gently traced a line down her cheek.

"Thank you for today. I enjoyed our time together."

"Me too," Emily said, suddenly shy.

Jeremiah's lips turned upward in a smile that weakened Emily's knees. "And thank you for your efforts with Ma. I know she can be difficult, but it seems as though you've won her over."

Barely able to concentrate, Emily shivered.

"Want to tell me how you managed it?" he asked, his voice hardly more than a whisper as he stared down into her eyes.

"Your ma's a good woman," Emily said. "She just needed to know I care about you. No mother is willing to stand by and watch her child be hurt."

He stepped closer, sliding his hands about her waist and drawing her to him. "And do you?"

Emily's breath caught in her throat at the rush of emotions swelling inside of her. Mrs. Thomas's warning echoed in her head. "Never let a man know how much you love him. It gives him the advantage over you. Keep the marriage on your terms."

She smiled, pushing aside the annoying inward voice.

"I care more than you could know, Jeremiah." Joy sprang to his eyes, bolstering her courage. "I've loved you since we were children. You've no idea the many times I dreamed you'd call on me."

Bewilderment flashed in his eyes. "You've loved me. . . ." He shook his head. "I was such an idiot. It never occurred to me back then that you would think I'm good enough for you."

"Good enough?" Emily frowned. "You mentioned that during the blizzard too. Why wouldn't I think you're good enough?"

A look of disbelief crossed his face, and he gathered her into his arms. "Emily, I should have known better. Look at all the years I wasted feeling like I couldn't measure up to your family because of my pa."

Emily gave a short laugh and pulled away enough to meet his gaze. "Jeremiah, no one measures up to my family. Not even me. But none of that matters. The only thing that matters is I love you."

She gasped at her sudden admission. Jeremiah had never spoken of love. It was rather bold for her to be the first one to bring it up.

He brought his forehead to rest upon hers. "Emily Daniels, the best thing that ever happened to me was that blizzard trapping you in my store. I was too dumb and stubborn to ever admit how I felt about you—how I feel."

"H—how you feel?"

A streak of lightning split the sky, followed by a loud clap of thunder. Emily jumped, barely containing a scream.

Jeremiah released her suddenly. "Come on. Let's go. We'll talk about this later."

Emily nodded and accepted his assistance into the wagon. Jeremiah trotted to the other side. He flapped the reins and headed toward home just as the rain started to fall.

By the time they reached the farm, they were soaked. But that was the least of their problems. The wind had grown to such an intensity, Emily could barely keep her footing against the gusts.

She started toward the house, but Jeremiah grabbed her. "The cellar," he yelled.

Nodding, she turned, but his fingers tightened on her arm. She pivoted back around.

There was no time for more talk! Then realizing he intended to see that she made it to the cellar, Emily yanked her arm away. "Go get your ma. I'll be all right."

He hesitated, clearly torn.

Rising on her toes, Emily kissed him hard on the lips. "Go!"

With a nod, he gave her arm a squeeze and dashed toward the house.

As she reached the cellar door, images flashed through her mind of when she was just a girl. A twister had demolished their barn and forced the family underground for the night.

She stepped into the musty cellar, shuddering at the terrifying memory.

"Keep us all safe, Lord. Please. Watch over my family and all of our friends and neighbors." She kept her focus on the door above her, waiting for Jeremiah to appear with Mother Daniels. She breathed a sigh of relief when they appeared after what seemed like an eternity.

"Emily! Help me get Ma down the steps."

Together they got his mother settled without too much difficulty. Jeremiah closed the doors and set the latch, then they listened grimly as the storm raged above them.

A deafening roar grew louder. A shudder claimed Emily. She knew the sounds of a tornado.

Jeremiah's face remained clouded with worry as the minutes ticked by. Emily reached forward and slipped her hand in his. She leaned her head against his shoulder and closed her eyes; and though she'd meant to make him feel better, she found that she was the one taking comfort from his nearness. He reached up and cupped her head with his opposite hand, pressing her closer.

"I don't have a very good feeling about this," he said.

Emily wished she had words to reassure him, but she heard the banging outside. That twister had gone right over them. If they were fortunate, only the barn was taken. But dread knotted inside of her. And when finally a deafening silence replaced the howl of the angry winds, her fears were confirmed. There was not a building standing on the Danielses' farm. No house. No barn.

Nothing but rubble.

ঽ

Jeremiah held back tears of frustration, anger, and helplessness as he stood next to the broken boards strewn across the land where his store had once stood. *Why, Lord? First my home and now my business? I don't understand why.* The only possessions left to him were the horses and his wagon, which had somehow been miraculously spared.

He glanced resentfully across the street. None of those buildings had been touched. Emily's Place stood without so much as a missing shingle; while Jeremiah's, the livery stable, and the hotel were all flattened. Other buildings had suffered damage as well.

Emily stood silently by his side. After the storm, they'd driven over to check on the St. John ranch and found the twister hadn't reached them at all. They'd endured a storm, but nothing had been damaged. They hadn't lost even one single chicken.

Emily's ma and pa had graciously extended an invitation to Jeremiah's ma; and after making sure she was settled comfortably, Jeremiah and Emily had headed to town.

"Jeremiah," Emily said quietly. "We still have the land. We can rebuild."

Shaking his head, Jeremiah crouched down and released a can of bootblack from beneath a board. "I don't have any money to start over. Everything was wrapped up in the store." The good news was that at least he'd managed to break even so far.

"Mr. Thomas will loan you the money to rebuild. Everyone knows what a wonderful businessman you are. The bank will be chomping at the bit to extend the loan."

He stood and faced her. Her sweet face softened him, and he smiled, suddenly happy that her store had been the one left standing. "No credit," he said, keeping his voice deliberately gentle. "My pa got us so deep in debt, Ma almost lost the farm after he died. I don't believe in buying something with someone else's money."

"Do you mean to tell me you paid cash to build your store?"

"That's right."

"But how?" she asked incredulously.

Jeremiah shrugged. "After we paid off the farm, I saved every extra penny over the years. Tuck gave me bonuses at

Christmastime and on my birthdays. Fifteen years of that adds up. Plus I sold off some cattle to Luke and Laney a couple of years ago when I decided not to raise them anymore."

A scowl scrunched her freckled nose and furrowed her brow. "Honestly, Jeremiah. If you could pay cash money, why didn't you buy Tucker's in the first place?"

Jeremiah stared at her, fighting the temptation to tell her exactly why. But as he studied the baffled expression on her face, he realized that she didn't know. She truly didn't. How could he tell her he was about to make an offer on Tucker's and offer her a wedding ring as well, when she swooped down and bought it out from under him with money she didn't even earn?

"I just didn't, that's all. Anyway, none of that matters now."

"But of course it matters, Jeremy! If you had bought Tucker's, you'd still have a store."

"Look, just let it go, all right?"

Hurt clouded her eyes and she turned away. She gathered a shaky breath, and Jeremiah knew she was fighting back tears.

"Emily. . .I didn't mean to sound curt."

"It's all right. I know this has been a difficult day. I suppose we'll stay in my old rooms over the mercantile?"

"You don't want to go home?"

She turned and gave him a blank stare. "Do you want to stay in the cellar? I guess I don't mind, but we'd be a lot more comfortable over the mercantile."

Jeremiah chuckled. "I meant I thought you'd want to stay with your folks."

"Do you want to?"

"No, I was going to stay in the wagon at the farm. I didn't even think about those rooms."

"We're blessed that we didn't lose everything, Jeremiah. I'm sure there are people who will be starting over with nothing. At least we still have Emily's Place, and it looks like we'll be able to salvage at least a small portion of your stock."

"I lost everything," he said flatly. "You didn't."

"But the store is ours. We'll get along nicely on what it brings in. You'll be able to rebuild the farm in no time. In the meantime, we can live upstairs."

Exasperated by her generous spirit, Jeremiah kicked a board. "Listen, you made yourself abundantly clear from the beginning of our marriage. Jeremiah's was mine, and Emily's Place was yours. We weren't to interfere in each other's business, remember? Well, I've honored my word so far, and I don't intend to go back on it now. I'll make a soddy on the farm and give up storekeeping. But know this, Emily, I'm not going to be supported by a woman. So any money you make will be yours to do with as you please. But not a penny of it will go to our living. Is that understood?"

"No! That's just silliness, Jeremiah. You love working in the store. You should run Emily's Place."

"I told you a long time ago I wouldn't work for you. And I'm not going to start now."

"Work for me? You'll be working for yourself. It's ours. Not mine. Things are different now, aren't they? We're married, and besides I was going to—"

"Don't pressure me, Emily. I said no."

Tears pooled in her eyes, and Jeremiah steeled himself, forcing his arms not to reach for her.

"Fine, Jeremiah Daniels. Be stubborn, then. I'm going to start supper for us. Shall I rummage through the rubble here for something to cook, or will you accept food from my store?"

Before he could answer, Emily put her hands firmly on her hips and leveled her gaze at him. "Will you please drive to the ranch and let our parents know we will be staying in town? And do me the courtesy of not humiliating me by sleeping in your wagon!"

She stomped off toward the mercantile, leaving him to stare after her. Unease gnawed his gut as he watched her. His mind whirled with the unbelievable events of the day. A day that had started with optimism had ended in destruction.

With a shake of his head, he cast another glance at the fallen store. His shoulders slumped. No matter how hard he tried, it seemed his pa's failures followed him like a curse.

With a heavy heart, he climbed into the wagon and headed toward the St. John ranch. Dread engulfed him as he tried to construct the words to tell his ma. Not only did she lose her home, but he had no means to support her in her old age. Tears stung his eyes once more, but this time he was powerless to rein in the onslaught of despair.

eighteen

Without giving it a second thought, Emily broke an ironclad rule for Sunday. She opened the store just in case folks needed supplies—and they did. Once the word spread, it seemed everyone in town headed for the store—if for no other reason than to assure themselves that their friends and neighbors were all right.

Hour after hour, the onslaught of customers continued. Until far into the night, Emily handed out blankets, lanterns, kerosene, and anything else folks were in need of. But, rather than profit on the Lord's Day, she extended credit to all; and they promised to pay her when they got back on their feet.

She wasn't alone in her vigil. Anthony opened the church, and Sam set up a small hospital for those in need of medical attention.

From all over the county, reports were coming in of damaged or destroyed homes and property. Some announced animals missing or killed, but not one report confirmed a death among Emily's friends and neighbors. Her heart sang with thankfulness for that. She blessed the Lord for sparing Emily's Place, and even the folks who had been unkind to her came and humbly accepted the goods she had to share.

For a town that had been divided by opinion only a day ago, Harper now united in a common cause—survival. Families who were barely on speaking terms before the storm now doubled up in still inhabitable homes. Few allowed pride to keep them from accepting help.

Emily breathed a sigh of relief when the last customer said farewell. She locked up and headed back through the store to take inventory of her depleted stock.

From time to time she paused in her work to glance anxiously at the clock. Jeremiah still hadn't returned. She hoped he'd eaten at her ma and pa's because she'd been too busy with the store to cook the promised supper. As the minutes ticked away, she began to worry in earnest. For the first time since her disappointing conversation with Jeremiah on the site where Jeremiah's once stood, she found the presence of mind to mull over the events of the day.

Oh, if only she'd torn up that contract before the storm hit. Now, there would be no convincing him. How could a Christian man be so stubborn as to scratch out a living on a farm when he could at least live comfortably with the profits from the store?

The thought of Jeremiah coming home each night, so exhausted he could barely drag himself to bed, filled her with despair. That wasn't the life for him. He was born to manage goods for sale.

A knock at the door pulled her from her musing with a jerk. Cautiously she made her way across the room and peered through the small window. She squinted and was able to make out a shadowy male form. "Jeremiah?" she called through the door.

"Let me in," came the muffled reply.

Relief welled inside of Emily.

She unlocked the door and threw it open. "It's about time. I was beginning to worry. . . ." Confusion clouded Emily's mind as a figure stepped from the shadows, and Mr. Gregory's dark face loomed before her.

"Where is she?" He grabbed her arm and pushed her farther into the store.

Every cell in Emily's body shook with fear as pain laced her arm. "Wh–who?"

A growl escaped his throat as he towered over her, his eyes narrowing. "You know who. My wife." He released her arm and shoved her toward the counter. "She's gone, and so are my daughters. I think you have something to do with it."

"Me? Mr. Gregory, I assure you, you're mistaken." He took another menacing step forward, his fists clenched. *Help me, dear Lord!*

"You and your ideas. Owning your own business and working when you should be having sons to carry on your husband's name. What kind of woman are you to encourage married women to go out and work?"

"I–I never. . . I only want women to have the right to do so, Mr. Gregory. I assure you, I would never encourage a woman to go out and work against her husband's will, particularly to the neglect of her family. I–I bought the store when I was single."

"A young woman has no business leaving her pa's home until she is married," he snarled, and Emily nearly wilted to the floor.

"Sir, I–I respect your opinions. Many share your view. But—"

"Shut up. Where is my family?"

"I'm sure I don't know where your wife and daughters are."

A sneer marred his face. For the first time, Emily noticed he swayed as he walked. Was he intoxicated? Although liquor was illegal in Kansas, everyone knew some folks made their own.

Surging toward her, Mr. Gregory muttered an oath, his arms reaching out. Emily stepped out of his way, easily evading his grasp. His face grew white, and he grappled at the air.

Emily gave a bewildered gasp as he crashed to the floor, taking out a display of newly arrived dime novels on the way down. "Help me," he said, though his words were barely discernable. For an instant, Emily froze, torn between the desire to run away and the knowledge that this man was hurt and needed her help—regardless of what had just occurred. She sent up a hasty prayer for protection and sank to her knees beside him. Blood trickled down his cheek from a gash at the side of his head, and she knew the wound was received before his fall. "Mr. Gregory. What happened?"

He groaned and mumbled something unintelligible.

"I'll be right back," she said, though she knew in all likelihood he couldn't hear her. "I'm going to go outside to the pump and bring some water to clean that wound. And we'll see about getting you to the church, where Sam can have a look at you."

She grabbed a pitcher and dashed out the door and around to the back of the store.

&

Jeremiah took the steps up to Emily's Place two at a time. Why was the door wide open? He strode inside, his heart nearly stopping at the disarray and the sight of Mr. Gregory sprawled on the floor. "Emily!" he called, terror gripping his gut. "Where are you?"

If Gregory had harmed one hair on her head—

"Emily!"

"I'm here, Jeremiah. Honestly, stop shouting before everyone in town ends up here." Jeremiah turned to see his wife coming through the door, carrying a pitcher of water.

"Oh, thank God, you're all right." He gathered her in his arms and held her tightly against him, mindless of the pitcher gouging into his stomach.

"Of course I am." His shoulder muffled her words.

He pulled back so he could look her in the eyes. Reaching forward, he stroked her face, then he bent and kissed her gently on her lips. "I was afraid Gregory might have harmed you."

"Why would you think that?" she asked, dipping her head toward the unconscious man. "He's the one on the floor."

Exasperated, Jeremiah released her and closed the door. "What happened here?"

"Not much, really. May I have your handkerchief, please?"

He fished the hanky from his pocket and handed it to her.

"Thank you." Emily knelt beside Mr. Gregory. She wet the cloth and gently began wiping away the blood from his face. "He must have been injured before he came over here, because one second he was coming after me, and the next he was on the floor."

"You're right. He was already injured."

Emily glanced up and arched a brow. "How do you know?"

He took her by the arm and pulled her to her feet. "Come to the storeroom with me, and I'll tell you."

It wouldn't do for Mr. Gregory to gain consciousness and hear what Jeremiah had to say. Once they were out of earshot, Jeremiah gathered a breath. "I found Mrs. Gregory and her girls walking outside of town. Mrs. Gregory was badly beaten and could barely walk without assistance. I took her to your ma and pa."

Revulsion covered Emily's features. "Did Mr. Gregory. . . ?"

Jeremiah nodded grimly. "He was angry that the hotel was flattened; and when she suggested maybe she could take in laundry to help them get back on their feet, he went crazy and started hitting her."

"Oh, my." She glanced up at Jeremiah. "Is Mrs. Gregory all right?"

"She will be. Physically. But that woman has deep wounds on the inside of her too. Emotional wounds that only God can heal."

"What will she do?" Emily asked. "Will she go back to him?"

Jeremiah shrugged. "Your pa and ma offered her and the girls the use of the old soddy until she decides what's to be done."

"And Mr. Gregory? What should we do about him?"

Anger burned a fire inside of Jeremiah at the memory of poor Mrs. Gregory's bruised and bleeding face. "We should dump the no-account in the street and let him take his chances, but I suppose we'd better load him into the wagon and cart him over to the church so Sam can doctor him."

Emily shuddered. "Let's do it, then. The sooner we get him out of the store, the better as far as I'm concerned."

The next morning Sam reported Mr. Gregory had left before dawn.

 &

A week later, the town still looked like a great battle had been waged on Main Street. The desolation was phenomenal; and according to Amelia Bell, even she could find no pleasure in the fact that she had all the news stories she could report and then some. Several families had had enough of the volatile Kansas weather and were packing up anything they could salvage and heading back to wherever they'd come from.

The tried-and-true prairie-dwelling Kansans stiffened their upper lips. They'd suffered through blizzards, crop failures, prairie fires, pestilence, and droughts. A twister would not get the better of them. And that was the crux of the talk around the cracker barrels at Emily's Place—which had become the town central.

The store was packed from open to close every day. Only one person remained absent, filling Emily with emptiness even in the midst of the crowded mercantile: Jeremiah.

Each night he slept on a cot in the storeroom, and every morning he rose before dawn and left for the farm, working until dusk.

Emily knew they couldn't go on this way; but for the life of her, she didn't know how to make things better, so she prayed and cried and prayed some more, hoping desperately that God would soon hear her plea and send help.

nineteen

Sunday morning dawned bright, promising to be the warmest day of the year thus far. Emily walked beside Jeremiah as they made their way to the church. Her eyes grew wide at the congested churchyard. She'd never seen so many wagons, indicating a full service.

"Jeremiah, look!" Emily's heart sang at the sight of Mother Daniels leaning heavily on her walking stick with Jack on one side of her and Will on the other. Emily's brothers made a gallant attempt to pretend to be fighting for the honor of escorting her, but anyone could tell they were ensuring she made it to the church without stumbling.

"Good morning, Mother Daniels!" Emily said. "It's wonderful to see you. You're getting along so well."

"That I am," she replied. "Doc says I'll probably have to use this for the rest of my life, but at least I can walk on my own."

She turned to her escorts. "You two run along. My boy is here to take care of me, now."

Will grabbed his chest in mock offense. "Come on, Jack. I think we've been jilted."

Mother Daniels shook her head as she watched Emily's brothers race toward the church. "Those two make my head spin." She turned to Jeremiah. "And why haven't you been over to see your ma this week?"

Jeremiah bent and kissed her cheek. "I'm sorry. I've been busy."

Mother Daniels studied his face, her eyes clouded with concern. "You feeling poorly, Son?"

"He's been working too hard trying to clean up at the farm," Emily broke in, earning her a scowl from her husband. She didn't care. If anyone could reason with him, it was his ma.

Mother Daniels's face grew pensive, then she shifted her gaze between Jeremiah and Emily. "How about if the three of us take a trip to the farm after services?"

Emily's stomach churned at the thought of having to witness the devastation again, but she didn't have the heart to say no to the woman who obviously needed to see her home. She smiled. "I made a nice ham yesterday. I'll slice it and pack a picnic."

Mother Daniels's face brightened. "Sounds wonderful." She moved slowly up the steps ahead of them.

Jeremiah leaned close and whispered in Emily's ear. "I guess I have no say in the matter."

"I guess not," Emily retorted, then turned to smile brightly at Anthony as they entered the church.

❧

Jeremiah watched the look of sorrow pass over Ma's face as she witnessed the destruction of her home for the first time since the storm. "I'm sorry, Ma," he said, lifting her from the wagon. Ma accepted her walking stick from his hand and silently walked toward the site where her house once stood.

Turning to Emily, Jeremiah reached out to help her down. She placed her hands on his shoulders, and his senses reeled at her nearness. The scent of soft lavender drifted over him as she slid into his arms. He was nearly overcome with the desire to pull her close and bury his face in the curve of her neck.

She stared up at him. "I miss you," she whispered. She rose on her toes and pressed a soft kiss to his lips. Jeremiah tightened his hold, but she resisted, pulling gently from his arms. "Go see to your ma. She's not steady enough on her feet to walk through that rubble alone. I'm going to get the lunch ready."

Reluctantly, he let her go and strode to his ma's side. He cleared his throat. "I've managed to save a few things, Ma, but not much."

She shook her head. "It doesn't matter." She turned to him

suddenly. "I want to sell it."

Jeremiah blinked. "What?"

"Myra Hastings came to see me a few days ago. She's answered an advertisement for a position as headmistress at a girl's school in Boston. You know she went to college before her pa forced her to move here."

"I'm sure you'll miss her." Jeremiah shifted. Did Ma want to move off too?

"I'm sure I will, but that isn't the point. She will need to sell the boardinghouse, and I'd like to buy it."

"And you'd have to sell the farm in order to do that." Jeremiah's gut clenched. How could she even consider selling their home? Without the farm, he would be forced to accept his wife's charity or live at the boardinghouse with his ma. The thought of either gnawed at him. "Are you sure that's a good idea?"

"Yes. I know you should have the right to your pa's farm; but if you're honest, you'll admit farming isn't in your heart. You've only kept it going for me all these years. I'm grateful, but you don't need it, and I do."

"I understand, Ma. But I was going to rebuild and move back out here."

"There's no need for you to do that, and it doesn't make real good sense to consider such a thing. You and Emily are townsfolk. You have your store; and if you don't want to live above the mercantile, use the land where your store was and build a house."

"But why do you want to move to town when I could rebuild your home? It's home. All our memories are here."

Ma released a heavy sigh. "Oh, Jeremiah. The memories here are not good. Your pa and his tirades and beatings, then after he died, memories of my young son working to take care of me. I'd like to start a new chapter, and maybe I can help someone in the process."

"What do you mean?"

"Mrs. Gregory and her girls need somewhere to live, and I need someone to help me run the boardinghouse. Mrs. Gregory and I have traveled the same road. We understand each other and will get along very nicely. It's a good arrangement."

"And what happens if Mr. Gregory comes back?"

She shrugged. "We'll have to deal with that if it happens. But for now, this plan just makes good sense."

"What makes sense?"

Jeremiah turned. The sight of Emily's sunny face reminded him of his options. He groaned inwardly. How could he live off his wife's charity? "Ma wants to sell the farm and buy the boardinghouse."

"Why, that's a marvelous idea!"

Ma chuckled. "And guess who would be Harper's new businesswoman?"

Tossing back her head, Emily burst into peals of laughter and hugged Ma close. "Well, rest assured, my days of giving speeches and going to rallies are over. You may take my place. I'm sure Mrs. Thomas would be thrilled to have you."

Joining in the laughter, Ma shook her head. "No, thank you. We women may have the right to vote someday, but I don't think I'm quite up for joining the suffragists. I'll leave bloomer outfits and cigar smoking to Mrs. Krenshaw."

Emily suddenly turned to Jeremiah. "What do you think of your ma selling the farm, Jeremy?"

Jeremiah exulted in the pleasant way his nickname rolled from her lips. He received it as an endearment and his pulse quickened. "I don't really know. I suppose I'll have to let the idea grow on me. It's really Ma's decision to make."

"I was just trying to show him how much sense it makes when you walked up. Since that crazy contract is no longer between you two, Jeremiah can run the store. He doesn't need this farm."

"What do you mean, the contract is no longer between us?"

Mother Daniels cleared her throat as Emily gave her a long

look, her eyes speaking volumes that Jeremiah was helpless to read.

"Take me to the ranch," Ma said. "Then you two can discuss this in private."

"But what about lunch?"

She shrugged. "Eat while you talk for all I care. But it's time you work some things out. It's obvious to anyone that you love each other desperately. If any two people are meant to be together, it's you. I've known that since you were children."

"So have I," Emily said, eyes shining.

A lump lodged in Jeremiah's throat at her admission. "Emily...," he began, but Ma interrupted.

"Take me home so I can rest this aching leg. Then you can work it out between you."

The women strode arm in arm, leaving Jeremiah to follow in stunned silence. He had a feeling the upcoming discussion with his wife might just be the most important of their lives.

❧

"Now, what's this about tearing up the contract?" Jeremiah demanded. They had made sure Mother Daniels was settled, declined an invitation to lunch from Emily's ma, and were now headed back to town. Still, Emily was surprised he'd brought it up so suddenly.

"Well, that's what the picnic was about, but the storm came before I could give you the document to tear up. I started to tell you while we were standing in the rubble of Daniels's, but you wouldn't hear me."

"I'm sorry, Em. I've been acting like an idiot all week. I've just had trouble trying to figure out exactly what God has in mind. It's not easy, losing everything in one day."

Emily pressed his hand with hers. "Oh, Jeremiah. You didn't. Don't you see? You still have a place to live, a business to run."

He snorted. "A home and a business that are yours."

She raised her hands helplessly and let them drop to her lap. "Jeremiah, haven't you learned anything from me? Men have been sharing with their wives since the dawn of time. Why can't you take what I have to offer? Eventually, you can use your land across the road from Emily's to build us a nice home. For now, let me share the store with you. You were willing to marry me for it at one time, why not just take it now? It doesn't matter to me anymore."

Glancing at her sharply, Jeremiah drew a breath and pulled the wagon to the side of the road. He wrapped the reins around the brake and turned to her. "What do you mean, I was willing to marry you for it? That never crossed my mind. It was you I wanted—not the store. I still had my store at the time."

Emily gathered a shaky breath. "Oh, Jeremiah, let's not start this off with lies. I'll be honest first." Her voice faltered, and tears threatened to choke her words; but she knew she'd gone too far to turn back now. "The night of the harvest dance, I heard you and Harold Baxter discussing who would be the first to marry me and run my store."

The blood drained from Jeremiah's face. He reached for Emily, and she went to him willingly, for she had no strength to resist.

"Honey, you misunderstood. I promise you, that's not what I meant. Harold, yes. But not me. I just meant I planned to court you. Do you remember the day you got the letter from your grandmother's attorney?"

Emily nodded against his chest.

"Before you read it, I was trying to work up the nerve to ask your permission to call on you."

She pulled away and met his gaze, unable to deny the earnestness she saw in his eyes. "You were?"

"Yes. I planned to talk to Tucker about selling the store to me, since I knew he wanted to sell. I wanted to have something to offer you before I courted you. I was going to ask you to marry me inside a month."

Horror widened her eyes. "And I ruined everything!"

"I wouldn't exactly say everything was ruined," he drawled. "God still worked out a way to get us together."

"Jeremiah, if I had known how much you wanted Tucker's, I never would have bought it. I just didn't know you had the money to buy it. I only bought it in the first place to be close to you and because. . .because I wanted to do something. . . ."

She stopped. She had never spoken of her feelings to anyone before. In all the years of being surrounded by fantastic St. Johns, she'd withheld the fact that she felt practically nonexistent.

Grabbing her hands, Jeremiah shifted closer to her on the seat. "You only wanted to do what?"

Tears stung her eyes at his gentle concern. She had said she'd start by being honest with him—but what if he agreed that she wasn't special like the other members of her family? It was one thing to quietly hold onto that belief, quite another to give someone the opportunity to agree.

"Don't cry," he soothed. "You can tell me anything."

Deciding to trust his love for her, Emily opened her mouth and a flood of words began. "It's just that everyone in my family is so handsome and good at everything. Everyone except me, the adopted one. I just. . .Jeremiah, I just wanted to be good at something. I knew I could never be a great beauty like the other girls, but for once I wanted to do something well. I just thought if I ran the mercantile well, maybe people would see that I'm not the only St. John who doesn't amount to anything. I guess that's why I joined the Suffrage Association. I just wanted to do something special."

Jeremiah released her hands. Gently, he cupped the sides of her neck, forcing her to meet his gaze. "Now you listen to me. First, I don't know where you got the idea that you're not special, but you are. Who is the only teacher in Harper to get a teaching certificate from normal school?"

Emily smiled. "Me."

"Right. Folks around here think that's pretty special. And

who set this town on its ear by giving the two best speeches ever heard in Harper?"

"I wouldn't go that far," she said with a wry grin.

"I would. You're an amazing woman, without even knowing it. You do whatever you set out to do, and you do it well. Even my ma is talking about wanting votes for women. Now, who else but a special woman could have won her over?"

A giggle escaped her lips, then she sobered. "I guess I just need to know there's a purpose for me."

"What makes you happy? That's usually a pretty good indication of what God planned for you."

Her cheeks warmed, but she held his gaze, determined to keep her resolve to be completely open with this man she loved. "I've never been happier than the weeks I stayed home and cooked and cleaned for you, Jeremiah. All I've ever wanted was to be near you. It means more to me than running a successful store or votes for women or anything else for that matter, except my relationship with God."

He kissed her then, without saying a word. His mouth moved slowly over hers. Breathless, she clung to him by the time he pulled slightly away.

"I love you," he whispered against her lips, sliding his hands down her neck and arms and finally gathering her around the waist. He cuddled her close and deepened his kiss once more, lingering, leaving Emily's senses reeling by the time he pulled away.

"My purpose in life has never been clearer, Emily." His husky voice sent a shiver down her spine.

"What makes you happy?" she whispered, her lips still tingling from his kiss.

"You should already know the answer to that question, by now."

"Running the store? You're not a farmer."

He grinned. "It's what I do best. It gives me satisfaction at the end of the day to know that's something I can do well.

But that's not what makes me happy."

"What then?"

"Knowing that God handpicked us to be together." His gaze held her tenderly. "We've wasted a lot of time with stubbornness and misunderstanding. I think it's time to put all that behind us and move forward."

"And you'll let me share the mercantile with you?"

"Yes, we'll run it together."

"Until the children come along. Then I'll stay home and take care of them."

"If that's what you want." A smiled played at the corners of his mouth. "Did you mean what you said about not going to any more rallies?"

"Yes. I hope women have the vote soon. We deserve it. I realize now that I took up a cause because I was looking for a place to fit in. But I don't need the Suffrage Association anymore. I know where my place is." She smiled at him, feeling for the first time in her life that she truly belonged. "With you."

Jeremiah pressed an urgent kiss to her lips. "Then let's go home."

A Letter To Our Readers

Dear Reader:

In order that we might better contribute to your reading enjoyment, we would appreciate your taking a few minutes to respond to the following questions. We welcome your comments and read each form and letter we receive. When completed, please return to the following:

Fiction Editor
Heartsong Presents
PO Box 719
Uhrichsville, Ohio 44683

1. Did you enjoy reading *Emily's Place* by Tracey Victoria Bateman?
   ❏ Very much! I would like to see more books by this author!
   ❏ Moderately. I would have enjoyed it more if

   _____

   _____

   _____

2. Are you a member of **Heartsong Presents**? ❏ Yes ❏ No
   If no, where did you purchase this book? _____

   _____

3. How would you rate, on a scale from 1 (poor) to 5 (superior), the cover design? _____

4. On a scale from 1 (poor) to 10 (superior), please rate the following elements.

   ____ Heroine   ____ Plot
   ____ Hero   ____ Inspirational theme
   ____ Setting   ____ Secondary characters

5. These characters were special because?_____

   _____

   _____

6. How has this book inspired your life?_____

   _____

   _____

7. What settings would you like to see covered in future
   Heartsong Presents books? _____

   _____

   _____

8. What are some inspirational themes you would like to see
   treated in future books? _____

   _____

   _____

9. Would you be interested in reading other **Heartsong
   Presents** titles? ❏ Yes   ❏ No

10. Please check your age range:
    ❏ Under 18   ❏ 18-24
    ❏ 25-34   ❏ 35-45
    ❏ 46-55   ❏ Over 55

Name_____

Occupation _____

Address _____

City_____ State_____ Zip_____

Minnesota

*I*n 1877, the citizens of Chippewa Falls, Minnesota, are recovering from the devastation of a five-year grasshopper infestation. Throughout the years that follow, countless hardships, trials, and life-threatening dangers will plague the settlers as they struggle for survival amidst the harsh environs and crude conditions of the state's southwest plains. Yet love always prevails.

Historical, paperback, 480 pages, 5 ³/₁₆" x 8"

❤ ❤ ❤ ❤ ❤ ❤ ❤ ❤ ❤ ❤ ❤ ❤ ❤ ❤ ❤ ❤ ❤

Please send me _____ copies of *Minnesota* I am enclosing $6.99 for each. (Please add $2.00 to cover postage and handling per order. OH add 6% tax.)

Send check or money order, no cash or C.O.D.s please.

Name _____

Address _____

City, State, Zip _____

To place a credit card order, call 1-800-847-8270.
Send to: Heartsong Presents Reader Service, PO Box 721, Uhrichsville, OH 44683

❤ ❤ ❤ ❤ ❤ ❤ ❤ ❤ ❤ ❤ ❤ ❤ ❤ ❤ ❤ ❤ ❤